21 Years of Jane

In Loving Memory of Aurea Arroyo

For Brittany Evans and Summer Slevin

One

I was sitting on the front porch of my parents split level ranch house, my hands shielding my eyes from the sun, waiting for … I reached into my jacket pocket and pulled out the folded piece of paper; *Nolan.*

His family had just moved to Paris, Ohio and our parents insisted that we become friends. Mostly my parents since I was something of a loner. They wanted to see me out and about doing normal things but I wasn't normal and they didn't seem to want to accept it.

I sighed as I shoved the paper back into my pocket and leaned back in my chair, closing my eyes. Although I didn't like the sun's rays blinding me, I didn't mind the feel of its warmth against my face. I didn't realize I had fallen asleep, until I felt someone shaking me gently.

"Huh?" I asked, startled.

"You fell asleep, Starr," my mother said gently.

"Oh. Sorry," I mumbled shifting in my chair and running my hands through my mahogany colored bob. I wasn't proud of anything on my body, but I especially loved and took care of my hair; to me it was the only pretty thing I had to show off. "Did Nolan show up?"

"Yes," a deep, smooth voice replied.

I looked at my mother in confusion. The smile on her face and the wander of her eyes to the left, led me to see who had answered. While I managed to keep an uninterested look on my face, my heart felt like it was going to beat out of my chest. He had to be the hottest thing walking planet Earth these days and he was sitting on *my* porch. Big emerald green eyes, light brown shaggy hair, and a half smile that if I saw enough times, I'm sure would command me to get up and walk again.

"I'm going to go inside. You kids have fun today," my mother said as she walked back into the house.

I groaned inwardly. I wasn't a *kid.* My twenty-first birthday was in three and a half weeks, and she still treated me like I was a baby.

I heard Nolan's good-natured laughter and forced myself to smile. It was obvious that *he* wasn't a kid either. Not with a strong face like his, not with those arms, not with the way that shirt was hugging his chest ...

I sighed and folded my hands on my lap.

No reason to daydream about things that can't happen, Starr.

"So, how long was I out?" I asked with a nervous laugh.

"About ten minutes. At least that's how long I've been sitting here," he replied with that half smile. *Did he have dimples? Of course he did.*

"Sorry."

"No, it's okay. I didn't mind. You looked so peaceful, that I almost fell asleep just watching you," he said with a chuckle.

I smiled and felt a small blush starting to creep across my face, so I cleared my throat and looked away. I turned slightly in my chair when I heard the blinds move and rolled my eyes when I saw my little brother and sister sitting in the window watching us with big, goofy grins.

"We should probably go," I said loudly.

The two of them burst into giggles and I heard my mother chastising them for eavesdropping. More like spying, but I'd let them have this small victory. When I got home, it would be all out *Nerf* Gun war.

From where Nolan was sitting, I was pretty sure he couldn't see my chair for what it really was and I suddenly felt very self-conscious. My parents had a special table built for me to hide the bulk of it so I would go outside once and a while and get some fresh air.

Nolan got to his feet and smiled, "What did you want to do today?"

"I'm in a wheelchair," I blurted out.

He raised an eyebrow and without missing a beat replied, "Which I'm sure is cooler than my car, so maybe we should take your ride instead today."

I raised an eyebrow at him and his half smile turned into a full grin. Nolan walked over to me and pushed the table to the side. Then he grabbed one of the chairs that was sitting next to me and settled into it across from me.

He leaned back in the chair and crossed his hands behind his head.

"Can I ask what happened?"

"Legg–Calvé–Perthes Disease," I replied simply.

"Say what?" he asked.

"Layman's terms?" I asked. He nodded. "My blood flow sucked when I was 12, the ball on my femoral pretty much died and fell off. Then newer bolder, blood decided it would be a good idea to attack the necrotic bone so that it could get better. Of course, that plan backfired and I lost a ton of bone mass but I also gained new wheels because of it," I explained with a shrug.

"I had to learn how to walk again once. I could show you how some day," he said with a smile.

"That's kind of impossible. But I appreciate the thought."

"Nothing's impossible."

I stared at him for a moment, but didn't say anything. He seemed so upbeat about it that I couldn't crush his spirits.

But it *was* impossible for me to walk. Ever since I was twelve years old and my blood decided to stop flowing to my bones, I hadn't been able to walk since.

Honestly, I didn't mind sitting around all day. I didn't want an electric wheelchair so I would at least be able to get some kind of exercise in when I was out and about by rolling my wheels myself. My father once said that I could probably beat a 300 pound muscle man at an arm wrestling match.

"If you could walk anywhere in the world, where would it be?" he asked leaning to the left and placing a hand on his chin.

"The bathroom would be sufficient," I replied dryly.

Nolan started to laugh rather loudly. So loudly in fact that my little brother and sister took their places behind me in the window again to see what was going on.

"You might as well come out here and say hello, you little monsters," I called to them through the mesh screen.

I turned slightly and just in time to see them smile at each other and disappear from the window. The door burst open and my five year old brother and seven year old sister came barreling out the front door.

When they saw Nolan smiling at them, they immediately became shy, as small children tend to do when someone new is around, and walked over to my side, each tucking themselves under an arm.

"Aren't you going to say hi?" I asked them. They both looked up at Nolan from underneath my arms and waved shyly.

"Don't let them fool you," I said in a loud stage whisper. "These little monsters are quite the handful."

"Nuh uh!" my little brother shouted.

"Yuh huh!" my little sister shouted back at him.

"Told ya!" I said to Nolan with a wink.

Realizing that I had just proven my point, they both looked at me for a moment, before bursting into a fit of giggles.

Nolan grinned and leaned back in his chair again. Stella was the first to move slowly in his direction to inspect him. She pushed her little brown curls away from her face and put a hand on his arm. His grin melted into a warm smile as his emerald eyes met her sapphire eyes.

Stella's already won him over. The power of children, I thought shaking my head and smiling.

"My sister can't walk. But I still love her," she said to him.

For some reason, the innocence of her statement choked me up. The tears immediately blurred my vision and I could feel the lump in my throat.

"I love her too!" Liam insisted loudly, giving me a tight squeeze. I looked down at him and saw the pout on his face, thinking our sister's statement would make her somehow love me more than he did.

I put my cheek on the top of his soft blonde, straight hair and inhaled deeply. They both meant so much to me.

I only wish I'd told them more than I did.

"You can love her too if you want. Do you love Starr?" Stella asked Nolan with big eyes.

The tears dried up and I felt mortified. He didn't know me to even decide if he wanted to be my friend yet, and now he was getting cross examined by a seven year old that I just *knew* wouldn't let him skirt the question.

"Stella! Liam! Come inside now," my mom called stepping through the door.

They both ran toward the door but stopped and waved at Nolan and I before disappearing inside. I was fairly certain that my face was a deep shade of crimson, but I tried my best to look normal.

"Sorry about that," I said breezily.

"Hey, kids say the darndest things, don't they?" he asked with a laugh.

"That's an understatement," I replied rolling my eyes. I put my hands on the grips of my wheels and rolled myself to the edge of porch.

“Can you hand me that?” I asked pointing at the ramp that my father hadn’t had a chance to put in yet.

“We don’t need that. Hold on,” he said getting up and coming over to me. He put his hands on the handles of the chair and tilted me back. I looked up at him with wide, confused eyes but his reassuring grin managed to soothe half of the doubt. I knew what he was intending to do; I just didn’t think he could pull it off.

“I have two questions for you,” he said looking down at me with a grin. “The first one is what’s your real name?”

Bump.

We went down the first step.

“Jane,” I replied nervously as I gripped the sides of the chair tightly.

“Where the hell did Starr come from then?” he asked in confusion.

Bump, bump.

"Um. It was the first word I ever said. At least that's what mom and dad tell me. I used to go outside all the time and look at the stars when I was little. Now it takes everything inside of me just to be able to get out of bed."

Bump, bump, bump, bump.

"Fair enough," he replied.

"What's your second question?" I asked, still holding on for dear life.

"Was that so bad?" he asked with a smile, setting the wheels down on the pavement.

"Huh?" I looked around and saw that I was on the sidewalk now and off of the stairs.

Tricky, I thought with narrowed eyes.

"If we're going to be best friends, you're going to have to learn to trust me," he said coming to stand next to me.

I looked up at him and watched him slide his hands into his pockets with that half smile still planted on his face.

I was going to ask him exactly when I had agreed to be his best friend, when a car honking distracted me. I looked to my right and saw my father pulling down the street as he made his way toward the driveway.

I smiled and waved. He honked again and pulled in. When he stepped out of the car, I knew that Nolan would be intimidated; most people were. Dad was at least six foot five and he was built like a mountain. He believed that no matter what your age was, you should always try to stay in great physical condition, which worked well for him since he was a contractor. He closed the car door and walked over to us.

It was almost like looking into a mirror, with the exception of the gender difference. We had the same mahogany colored hair and hazel brown eyes. When we smiled the corners of our eyes crinkled and we had the same dimple in our right cheek.

"Hi Sweetheart!" he said happily as he stopped in front of me.

"Hi Daddy," I replied.

He leaned down and kissed me on the top of my head before straightening up and glancing at Nolan.

"Hello Mr. East," Nolan said extending a hand.

"Nolan," he replied firmly shaking his hand. "How did you get down? Did you use the ramp?" he asked me.

"No, he bumped me down the stairs," I explained.

"Let's not do that again, son," Dad said to him. "I don't want her to fall down and get hurt. It'll bring back bad memories."

"Yes sir," Nolan replied.

"Good. I'm glad we understand each other. Where are you two off to?" he asked, crossing his arms over his chest.

"I was thinking we'd go down to the park and maybe just hang out, but we haven't discussed it yet," I replied.

"Alright, well I expect you home by the time the sun goes down. Can you respect that?" he asked, switching his gaze back to Nolan.

"Yes sir," Nolan said again.

He's scared of Dad, just like I knew he would be, I though in amusement.

"Very good. You kids have fun," he said leaning down and giving me a hug before heading toward the house.

I rolled my eyes at being called a kid again and put my hands on the grips of the wheels. Nolan walked next to me as I rolled down the street and turned left at the end of the block. The park was more of a small patch of grass, a few swings, some slides, and a merry go round, but Stella and Liam loved it there. I almost felt bad for not bringing them with us.

But when I glanced up at Nolan as we turned the corner, the smile on his face washed all guilty feelings away.

Two

We got to the park about ten minutes later and I took my usual spot near a bench where I would sit and watch Stella and Liam play. Nolan sat down on the side closest to me.

"Starr?" he asked uneasily.

I looked at him.

He was so pretty that I couldn't help but smile.

"When your dad said that he didn't want you to relive bad memories from falling, what was he talking about?"

Oh.

The smile left my lips as I folded my hands in my lap and cleared my throat. I guess I'd tell him this story eventually anyway.

"Well, when I started my freshman year of high school, I had just gotten my wheelchair. My parents had spent all summer convincing me that I was normal and that having a wheelchair was nothing to be ashamed of. So that's how I went to school; thinking I was normal just like the other kids. My second week there, that theory was shot to shit in ways I never thought possible. See, I hadn't quite made any friends yet because I was shy so I spent a lot of time alone. I guess it made me an easy target," I said with a quiet chuckle. I pushed my hair back behind my ears and took a deep breath before I continued. "Anyway, I was late to class and the hallways were empty; or so I thought. A group of football players caught up to me and thought it would be a fun idea to see how fast my wheelchair could go. To be honest, I think they were drunk. I swore I smelled alcohol on their breaths, but I was too afraid to ever tell anyone. Come to think of it, you're the first person that knows that," I said, glancing at Nolan.

He smiled softly and put a hand on the arm of my wheelchair while he waited for me to continue.

"I'm pretty sure you can tell where this is going, but let me continue. The closest place to me was the gym so I put everything I had into my arms and wheeled like hell. But of course no matter how fast I went, I was no match for a group of jocks. They caught up to me in the gym, formed a jock circle around me, and flipped my wheelchair on its side. Know what the worst part was? Not one gym class was held that day. I spent the rest of the school day on my side in the gym, crying, humiliated, and hungry. After school let out, the cheerleaders came running in for practice. Most of them laughed at me, but the captain and co-captain ran over and helped me up. They shut the other girls up too and sent for the principal. After that joyous day, my parents yanked me out of school and homeschooled me for the rest of my high school career. I guess that incident is the main reason I'm a bit of an introvert," I finished thoughtfully.

Nolan was silent and looking at the small group of children that suddenly appeared by the slide.

“Are you okay?” I asked him.

He cleared his throat but didn’t say anything. Not at first, so I let my eyes wander to the children as they took turns going down the slide and I smiled.

I really found myself wishing that Stella and Liam were with us. So much so, that I was moments away from taking my out my phone and texting them to bring them down, but Nolan finally spoke.

“I don’t understand how people can be so cruel.”

“Oh it was a long time ago. My parents just worry that it’ll happen again, but they also want me to make friends. It’s kind of a catch 22.”

"Well, I've shown you mine, now show me yours," I said cheerfully.

Nolan looked at me and raised an eyebrow.

"You said you had to learn to walk again once. What happened?"

"Oh!" He gave me a sheepish grin which caused me to blush, but I leaned toward him and rested my face in my hand while he talked. "I was a wild little kid, I guess you could say. I liked to run, scream, ride bikes, skateboard, rollerblade; you know the usual things kids like to do." I nodded even though I had never done half of those things. Come to think of it neither had Stella or Liam. "Anyway, so I thought I was a real bad ass when I was nine years old. I got this bright idea one day to see if I could go faster on a skateboard if I wore a rollerblade on my other foot. Needless to say, I didn't get very far. I fell down a concrete staircase near my mom's office building; got a compound fracture of it both of my legs. The docs looked at the X-Rays and said I'd be lucky to walk normally again, let alone walk at all. My mom cried her eyes out for weeks about it. Every time she saw me in the casts she would put a hand to her mouth and walk out of the room blubbering. The day I got the casts taken off, I remember thinking that my legs looked normal so why shouldn't I be able to use them, right? The doctor wound up giving me those metal crutches with the arm cuffs and told me that I would only ever be able to walk using them." Nolan gave me the power of the dimpled half smile, "Do you see crutches anywhere?"

I laughed and shook my head.

"I guess I was as determined as I thought I was cool. Which is why I say to you, my dearest Jane, that if I was able to get on my feet again, so shall you," he said with a grand arm sweeping gesture.

I looked down at my legs for a moment, honestly believing that I might be able to use them one day. But being a chronic pessimist as of late, I pushed the thought out of my head as quickly as it entered.

I shrugged in response and his smile faltered a little.

"Wanna try something?" he asked suddenly.

"Sure," I replied turning my attention back to the children who had now moved their enthusiasm to the swings. I smiled wistfully; it looked like a lot of fun.

Nolan got up from where he sat and got behind me. He put his hands on the wheelchair handles and began to push me toward the children. I tilted my head up to look at him. He looked a bit mischievous and a bit determined. He left me at the edge of the dirt pit that housed the swings and the slide. I watched him walk over to the children and start negotiations of some sort.

One of the little boys, no older than eight years old, hopped off of his swing and gave Nolan a high five. Then they both made their way to where I was sitting, watching them curiously, and the little boy gave me as big a smile as Nolan had on his face.

"What's going on?" I asked them suspiciously.

"Xavier here wants you to have his swing for a little while," Nolan explained putting a hand on the little boy's shoulder.

I felt a tear sting my eye. Children didn't easily give up what they were enjoying and playing with and this little boy, who didn't know me from anywhere, was willingly giving up his swing.

"Thank you, but I can't swing," I said softly, wiping away a tear.

"Sure you can! We're going to help you!" Xavier exclaimed happily.

I looked up worriedly at Nolan who gave me a grin and reached down for me. I instinctively pushed his hands away and turned the wheelchair around. I started to wheel myself back toward the bench when Xavier's sad voice stopped me.

"She doesn't like me, huh?" he asked.

I stopped wheeling and turned myself to face them. The look on his face broke my heart; I felt like I had let him down in a way that seemed irreparable.

"I just don't know if I can," I explained quietly.

Xavier came over to me and with his big brown eyes simply said, "You'll never know unless you try."

I eyed him for a moment, blinking back fresh tears before I looked at Nolan and nodded. Nolan smiled and told Xavier to push my chair back toward the dirt pit and then he would take over from there.

When Xavier had me pushed firmly against the long wooden bars that were keeping the "clean" dirt in the playground, Nolan came around to the front of me and put a hand on either side of my chair.

“Trust me?” he asked as he leaned down.

“I don’t have much of a choice,” I replied with a nervous laugh.

He grinned and reached down for me. I wrapped my arms around his shoulders and closed my eyes as he gently lifted me out of the chair, careful to still leave my legs in a somewhat seated position. I heard Xavier’s feet as he ran through the dirt and straight to his swing. I glanced over and saw him standing behind it waiting.

“One sec and she’s all yours, buddy,” Nolan said to him.

Xavier moved to the side and Nolan sat me on the swing. I gripped the chains with every bit of strength that I had. I was terrified of falling off and what this would feel like without something supporting my back.

And that's when I felt Xavier's small hands on my back, holding me upright. Nolan winked at me and then helped Xavier stand on the swing to keep my legs held together tightly and to still give my back support.

"Ready?" he asked us.

"Won't this break with both of us on it?" I asked nervously.

"Jane, you can't weigh more than one hundred and ten pounds and Xavier can't weigh more than sixty pounds; no way will the chains snap. Now hold on tight guys!" he said as he gave us a gentle push.

We didn't go very far into the sky, but enough to make my heart flutter and Xavier squeal happily. Our bodies went back toward Nolan who gave us another gentle shove.

"Wanna go higher?" Xavier asked me.

"Um, sure," I replied, even though I didn't want to.

"Harder, Nolan!" Xavier called as we went back toward him again.

I heard him laugh as he gave us another gentle, but firmer push. This time we went up as high as the other children who were now cheering us on. After a few more times pushing us, I was ready to get off the swing. Xavier carefully climbed off keeping a small hand on my back the entire time.

"Did you have fun, Starr?" he asked me with a big smile.

"A lot of fun and it's all because of you," I replied over my shoulder.

Nolan came over and scooped me out of the swing.

"Hold on," I said to him. I looked at Xavier who was now standing with his hands in his pockets. "Thank you. I haven't been brave enough to do that in years and you being there to help me ... it made me feel safe."

He blushed and scuffed his foot on the dirt, “You’re welcome. Maybe we can play again some time.”

“Next time I’ll bring my brother and sister with me. You’ll have a lot of fun with them,” I replied with a smile.

“Okay. That sounds like a good idea. We’ve have to get going now. Bye Nolan! Bye Starr!” he said, as he and the rest of the children turned and ran from the park.

I smiled when Nolan set me back in my wheelchair.

“Thank you. I never would have tried to do that if it weren’t for you, too.”

“Did you have fun?” he asked with a twinkle in his eye.

I nodded and rolled myself back toward the bench.

“Stick with me, Jane! We’re going big places; first the swings, next the bathroom! Just you wait and see,” he said breezily.

I just laughed and shook my head.

Three

Mom, Dad, Stella, Liam, Nolan, and I were all seated at the dinner table. We all had plates full of food and were chatting conversationally. I, however, was more targeted on Stella. I was sure eventually she'd bring up her cross examination again and I'd jump in, change the subject, and save the day.

"Starr's birthday is almost here," she said to Nolan, twirling a finger in her curly hair. "We want to give her a party, but she doesn't want one. Would you come if we gave her a party?"

I rolled my eyes.

"I don't want a party, Rabbit," I said.

I had nicknamed Stella Rabbit when she was a baby. She was always so fidgety and constantly moving around. Seven years later, not a thing had changed.

"It would be a surprise, Starr. Duh!" she responded.

"It's a not a surprise, if she knows," Liam interjected reasonably.

"I wasn't asking you," she shot back.

"Don't yell at me!" he shrieked, throwing a piece of bread at her.

I sighed and put my face in my hands. World War 3 had just broken out with these two; again.

"Kids, either you settle down, or you go to your rooms. No dessert and straight to bed," my mother warned, raising a finger.

They immediately quieted down after sticking their tongues out at each other, of course.

Mom stepped out of the room to answer the ringing phone.

My father chuckled and shook his head. He glanced at me and threw a piece of bread. I raised an eyebrow and chucked it back. It missed him and landed on the floor behind him. With a mischievous smile, he broke another piece of bread and threw it at me.

I looked down at the bread in my lap, and looked up at him slowly. I gave him the look that told him that the challenge had been accepted.

Instead of breaking a piece off of the roll I had, I threw the entire thing at him and caught him square in the face.

I threw my arms up, victorious, as the kids and Nolan laughed. My father picked up the roll and pulled his arm back to let it fly back in my direction, when my mother walked in and took the roll from his hand.

"Honestly," she said shaking her head.

I wasn't sure what exactly had gotten into me at that moment, but I grabbed a roll out of the basket and threw it at my mom.

"Lighten up," I said as it hit her.

For a moment she looked shocked, then outraged, then calm. Then her shoulders began to shake and she started to laugh. I raised my eyebrows as I met my father's eyes and we both shrugged.

Mom had been a lot of fun when I was younger, but ever since I wound up in this wheelchair, she took extra precaution when it came to me.

Coming into the dining room and seeing my father wielding a piece of bread, must've looked like an assault waiting to happen to her.

"May I have my roll back, dear?" Dad asked holding out his hand. She handed it back to him still giggling.

Stella took that opportunity to bring up my impending birthday again. I watched her put her elbows on the table and insert her chin accordingly. She batted her eyelashes a few times and I had to stifle a giggle.

"So would you? Come to her birthday party?" she asked, giving Nolan her best, I'm-too-cute-for-you-to-say-no face.

"If you have a party, yes, I will be here," he replied with a grin.

"What if we don't have a party because she doesn't let us?" she wailed dramatically.

"Then I'll still be here," he reassured her.

Stella gave him a big smile and ran from her seat. She made her way around the table and put her tiny arms around him, giving him the tightest hug she could muster.

"Thanks Nolan!" she said into his arm.

"You're welcome," he said laughing, and returning her hug.

She pulled away from him and made her way over to me and climbed onto my lap. She carefully balanced herself as to not hurt me and pushed my hair away from my ear. Leaning close she whispered, "I think he loves you."

I pulled back wide eyed and stole a glance at Nolan to make sure he hadn't heard Stella's comment. If he had, he was careful not to let it show on his face. She gave me a kiss on the cheek, climbed off, and skipped back to her seat.

"Help me bring out dessert, Stella," Mom said as she grabbed the dirty plates.

"Can I help too?" Liam asked.

"Yes you can," she said to him. He got up excitedly and ran into the kitchen.

"Hold on, Mom. I can take the dishes," I said pushing away from the table and wheeling toward her.

"Oh sweetheart, you have company. It's not very polite to leave him with -- your father," she finished in a loud stage whisper.

"I'm sure us men will be just fine," Dad said with a smirk.

"See? Daddy's got it under control. Here, let me take those," I said pulling a stack of dishes out of her hand and placing them on my lap.

She smiled and pushed the doors open so I could go through them. I went over to the dishwasher and pulled it open.

"You don't have to do all that, you know," she said.

"It's okay. I don't mind. Besides, my arms work just fine," I joked, flexing one.

She laughed and shook her head as she went over to the impatiently waiting children. One by one, I loaded the dishes on my lap into the dishwasher, then the ones that were sitting on the counter.

Mom, Stella, and Liam left the room with dessert, while I continued putting dishes in. When I was sure I had them all, I closed the door and pressed the button.

I made my way to the doors and pushed them open, rolling through as quickly as I could. I winced when the doors flung back toward me and hit the back of my wheels.

Just another subtle reminder that you're not normal, I thought with a heavy sigh.

I rolled over to my spot next to Nolan. My parents and siblings were heavy into conversation over the birthday party I didn't want. I sighed again and he nudged me.

I looked at him and he raised an eyebrow. I just shook my head slightly and shrugged.

"So what did you kids do today?" my dad asked turning his attention back to us.

"Starr got on the swings," Nolan immediately answered.

I put my face in my hand and groaned inwardly. Although my father was the more relaxed of my parents, he wasn't going to be too happy to hear that I was out of my chair without him there.

"She did ... What?" he asked in shock.

"She got on the swings," Nolan repeated uneasily.

"How?"

"I helped her."

"Why would you do that? Do you know how dangerous that could be for her?" my father exploded.

"Um, with all due respect Mr. East, Starr seems like a big enough girl to make her own decisions. Also, I wasn't going to do anything that would harm her," Nolan replied.

"Yeah Daddy!" Stella chimed in.

My father shot her a warning look and she immediately quieted down.

"Nolan there are things you need to understand. The first thing is, we don't know you," my father said pointing his fork at him. "The second thing is that I think Jessie and I would know what's best for Starr. And lastly, if you can't respect that my daughter *cannot* be out of her chair without either one of us present, then I suggest you leave and never come back. We want Starr to have friends and your parents said you were an upstanding young man, but I will not allow you to put my oldest in danger."

"Dad!" I exclaimed in shock.

"No Starr, don't interrupt me please," he said holding up a hand. "Can you respect that, Nolan?" he asked him.

He was quiet for a moment before he looked my father in the eyes and spoke.

"Mr. East, do you know what one of her hopes is? To be able to walk to the bathroom. That seems trivial enough doesn't it? But we aren't confined to a wheelchair and not given the chance to try new things. I never knew that walking to the bathroom was something that's so easily taken for granted, did *you*?" he asked.

My father dropped his fork and excused himself from the table.

"Aaron, sit down," my mother said, quietly but firmly. "The boy has a point. We don't know *what* Starr can and can't do, because we don't let her try."

I looked at my mom rather proudly. She and my father almost never disagreed on anything when it came to their kids, but she was standing up for me. And for Nolan.

"What else do you want to do, sweetheart?" she asked me while simultaneously giving my father a dangerous look.

"Well, I would love to ride a rollercoaster someday," I said slowly. "Those always looked like fun. Maybe walk up the stairs so I can play with the kids in their room. Walk outside to get the mail instead of having to roll and use the gripper. I'd love to walk on the beach and feel the cool water underneath my toes, forming sandy footprints because I'm *standing* there. I'd give anything to be able to jump rope next to Rabbit instead of holding one end for her. I think it would be so much fun to be able to run and stand when I play catch with Nugget." I blinked back angry tears. "I'd do anything to be able to go out with you and Dad; walk side by side and not having you worry about me getting bumped into."

She smiled at me, "What else?"

"Listen, I know this sounds like a long shot, but I would love to get married one day. I'd love to be in a pretty white dress and *walk* down the aisle."

I suddenly felt an overwhelming sadness. Hopefully, I still had my whole life in front of me, but I knew that was something that had the slimmest chance of happening.

"Oh Janey," my mom replied softly, her eyes growing misty. "It'll happen. Even if I have to help you walk down the aisle myself."

I smiled at her and sniffled. I refused to cry. Though I was kind of impressed with the fact that I had almost cried three times that day.

"There's a great amusement park about an hour away from here. It opens tomorrow if you want to go," Nolan whispered in my ear.

I looked at him and smiled.

"I don't think Dad is going to let me go," I whispered back.

"Maybe the day after tomorrow then," he replied quietly with that half smile.

I grinned in response.

"You two should get married," Stella said.

We both turned to look at her and she had her face in her hands again. But instead of giving the too cute to say no to look, she was giving us an innocent look.

"Stella Giselle!" my mother scolded. "You don't say things like that. Now take your brother outside and go play. You've got thirty minutes before you have to take a bath and get in bed."

"She's just being a kid, Mrs. East. It's okay," Nolan replied with a laugh.

My mom nodded and smiled. She told my father to help her clean up in the kitchen and they were gone. Nolan and I were left sitting at the dining room table in silence.

"I should probably get home. My parents might be wondering where I am," he said getting to his feet.

"Here, let me walk you to the door," I said pushing back from the table.

He chuckled at my joke and I smiled. It was nice to finally find some humor in my situation. I rolled to the front door with Nolan following me. Once we reached it he opened it and hesitated before walking through.

"Do you ... want to hang out tomorrow? I can come by earlier and we can go to the zoo or something," he said nervously.

"Sure! That sounds like a lot of fun," I replied enthusiastically.

"Awesome," he replied smiling widely. "I'll come by around ten, okay?"

I nodded and smiled up at him. Maybe I finally found a friend. Maybe I found a reason to get out of the house more; away from more than just the front porch.

"I'll see you tomorrow then," he said softly.

"Okay."

Nolan bit his lower lip for a moment, before leaning down and kissing me gently on the cheek. He walked out the front door and descended the stairs without so much as a backwards glance.

I put a hand to my cheek and watched him disappear down the street. I smiled and felt myself trembling.

Maybe I found something more.

Four

When I went to bed that night, my mother held my chair while I pulled myself onto the bed. She helped me straighten my legs out and sat down on the edge of the bed for a moment.

"He seems like a good boy," she said thoughtfully.

"He's nice, I guess," I replied with a shrug.

She looked at me carefully for a moment, before she brushed my hair away from my face and kissed me on top of my head.

"Good night, Starr."

"Good night, Mom."

I closed my eyes and pulled the sheets up to my chin when she turned the light off. I opened my eyes again when I heard a pair of tiny feet skitter into my room.

I looked over and saw Stella smiling at me.

"Hi Starr," she whispered.

"Hi Stella," I whispered back. "What's up?"

"Can I sleep with you tonight?" she asked with big eyes.

"You know it's not going to be comfortable for you right?" I asked.

She nodded and crawled onto the bed. I put my hands down and began to shift over to give her room but she stopped me.

"I'll be okay right here," she said, lying down on a small sliver of the bed.

"But I don't want you to fall off," I argued, trying to push myself over again.

"Janey, this is *your* bed. You don't have to move over to make room for me. You can be normal with me like you were with Nolan. I'm your friend too," she said putting a tiny arm around my waist and snuggling into my side.

"Thanks Stella," I said putting my cheek on top of her soft curls. "I like that you're my friend."

"I'm your *best* friend," she corrected in a tired voice.

"Always," I whispered.

I was asleep in no time. I didn't dream that night, but having Stella's arm around me while I slept was more than enough for me.

I didn't want to have another dream where I was walking on the beach anyway. They always depressed me when I woke up and saw my chair waiting patiently near my bed.

When I woke up the next day, Stella was gone. I smiled and stretched then I reached for my chair. There was a folded piece of white construction paper on it with my name written in Stella's handwriting.

Dear Starr,

Thank you for letting me have a sleepover with you. I love you.

Stella

I smiled and took in a deep breath. Stella had just set the bar so high for today, that even Nolan wouldn't be able to top that.

Nolan.

I threw the sheets off and pulled myself into my chair. I forgot he was coming over and I didn't even know what time it was. The Lego clock I had in my room stopped working months ago, but I kept it because the kids gave it to me for my eighteenth birthday.

I rolled out of my room and down the hallway into the bathroom. I found my toothbrush and began the boring two minute routine of scrubbing my teeth.

"Starrrrrrr! Nolan is here!" Liam screamed from the front door.

I heard a small pair of footsteps go barreling toward the door and heard Nolan grunt as, who I can only assume was Stella, attempted to tackle him.

I grabbed a brush and began the arduous task of trying to get my hair to look decent. I always woke up with it standing out on all sides.

"Honey, are you about ready?" Mom asked sticking her head into the bathroom.

The brush in my hand, the frazzled look on my face, and the fact that half of my hair was still standing up, answered her question. She laughed and took the brush from my hand. She ran it under the faucet for a few seconds before brushing my hair down.

"Stella's telling Nolan all about your sleepover," Mom said as she continued to brush my hair.

"She left me a note this morning too," I replied with a smile.

"Yes, I've heard," Mom said. "There you go, honey. Your hair is no longer standing up."

"Thanks Mom," I said gratefully. "Um, can I ask you for a favor?"

"Sure."

"Can you run interference so I can get back to my room?"

She nodded and started to laugh. She knew that depending on where Nolan was sitting or standing for that matter, he would see me in my pajamas when I rolled by.

I watched her step gingerly out of the bathroom and waited for her go ahead. She reached a hand back into the bathroom and waved at me to go.

I rolled out as quickly as I could. Unfortunately someone had closed my door when I went to the bathroom. I looked over frantically and saw Liam sitting on Nolan's lap. I grabbed the door handle and pushed it open just in time to hear Nolan greet me.

"Hey Jane!" he called out.

I felt mortified and rolled into my room without answering. A few moments later, Liam burst through my door as I was pulling my shirt over my head with Nolan right behind him.

"He said *hello,* Starr," Liam said.

I was tangled in my shirt. Half of it was over my head and half of it was wrapped in my arms.

"Come on, buddy. Let's let her get dressed," Nolan said, retreating with Liam.

I can't believe he just saw me in my bra, I thought in humiliation.

I quickly went to my dresser and pulled out a black tank top and pulled it on.

"Mom!" I called out.

I would need her to help me get my shorts on. Was I really going to wear shorts? Of course I was. Why not? He had already seen me half naked. I reasoned that when he saw my legs he wouldn't run in terror.

"Yes, honey?" she asked peeking her head in my room.

I held up a pair of blue denim shorts and she smiled.

Mom came over and helped me put them on then she backed up and put her hands on her hips.

"I never thought I'd see the day."

"Well Liam just busted into my room when I was trying to pull my shirt off, so a few scars won't scare him away," I replied dryly.

"I'll have a little chat with your brother about privacy after you leave," she said meaningfully.

"Thanks Mom."

I took a look at myself in the full length mirror after she slid my sandals onto my feet and rolled out behind her.

Nolan was sitting in his original spot with Liam on his lap again. They were both listening to Stella going on and on about our sleepover.

"...and I told her that I'm her friend too and she said she was happy that I am," Stella was saying proudly.

"I'm your friend too, right?" Liam asked me as I entered the room and looking dangerously close to tears.

"Of course you are, Nugget!" (I called him Nugget because of how small he was.)

He stuck his tongue out at Stella and she opened her mouth to respond, but Mom quickly ushered them out of the room.

"Have a good day, you two!" she called out as she left us in the room alone.

Nolan glanced over at me when Mom disappeared, "Ready?"

"Yeah. Listen, I'm sorry about that. Earlier. In my room," I mumbled.

"Oh it's no big deal," he replied with a smile. "I mean, it's not like I was standing there ogling you or anything. I saw your predicament and I grabbed Liam and split."

Huh.

"So what are we doing today?" I asked, changing the subject and rolling toward the front door.

"I kind of like the zoo idea, if you're still up for it," he said following me out.

"Yeah, but that's a long walk from here. Unless you want to sit on my lap," I said with a laugh.

Nolan threw his head back and laughed at my comment. Then he reached into his pocket and pulled out a pair of keys.

"We're driving there today. But maybe we can do that another day," he teased.

I giggled and went toward the stairs. Once again, Nolan got behind me, tilted me back, and bumped me down the stairs. Only this time I wasn't afraid.

I trusted him not to drop me.

I looked up at his face as he carefully lowered me down the stairs and felt that strange flutter I felt when he kissed my cheek.

Go away, I thought to my feelings.

Nolan settled me onto the sidewalk and pushed me toward a sleek black, brand new Explorer.

"Um, I thought you said that my wheelchair was nicer than your car," I said incredulously.

He grinned, "It is. You can take it anywhere. This thing has to stay outside. Can you imagine me driving it through the mall or something?"

He opened the passenger door for me and leaned down, picking me up into his arms. Nolan held me firmly against him as he eyed the situation.

"How ...?" he asked sheepishly.

"Ass first," I replied with a smile.

He grinned and leaned into the truck with me, placing me on the seat. I leaned down and grabbed my scarred legs, hoisting them in.

Nolan put one foot on the passenger floor as he shifted my legs so that they would rest naturally, before closing the door and folding my chair. I glanced in the passenger side mirror as he opened the back of the truck and carefully slid my chair in. Once he was satisfied that it was secure, he closed the door and came around the driver's side.

He opened the door, hopped in, and grinned at me as he fastened his seatbelt. I returned his grin and fastened mine as well.

He checked his side view and rear view mirrors before he pulled away from the curb. We drove mostly in silence as he pulled onto the freeway.

"Um, the zoo isn't anywhere near the freeway," I said.

"I know," he replied with a wink.

"Then where are we going?" I asked him curiously.

"You'll see," he said mysteriously.

After half an hour of driving, I was starting to wonder where we could possibly be going.

When we crossed state lines into Pennsylvania, I wondered if he knew that crossing state lines with an unwilling person was a federal crime.

After another hour, I found myself no longer caring.

Nolan pulled off of the freeway and went straight for about a mile. We were sitting at the stop light when I finally asked him where we were.

"Well, I *am* taking you to the zoo; sort of. I was thinking about it this morning. Why just go to the zoo when we can go to the zoo *and* the aquarium?"

I felt a tiny flicker of excitement. I had forgotten about the aquarium and the last time I had been here I was five years old. I was very curious to see if anything had changed.

"I haven't been here in years!" I said excitedly.

"I know," he replied with a mischievous grin.

I raised an eyebrow at him and he laughed. "Stella told me."

I rolled my eyes and laughed with him. "She seems to be really interested in our friendship."

"Invested too," he added turning at the light and heading toward the parking lot at the end of the next block.

My excitement flared up again when I saw the sign for the Pittsburgh PPG Zoo and Aquarium.

"She just wants to make sure that she stays my very best friend," I explained.

Nolan pulled into the closest spot he could find to the front doors and put the car in park. He turned it off and looked at me.

"I'd never try to take her place as your best friend. Liam's either," he said leaning his head back and smiling.

"Good, because it would *never* happen," I replied sticking my tongue out at him.

Nolan laughed and unbuckled his seatbelt. I smiled and undid mine. I leaned my arm against the window and watched all the people going in and out of the zoo or aquarium. I couldn't wait to get out of the truck and be a part of it. And that's when I suddenly felt Nolan's hand on my leg.

I looked down at it, and then raised my eyes to his. He was giving me his earth shattering half smile, dimple set.

"Your hand is on my leg," I said.

"I know," he replied.

"Any reason why?"

"I just wanted to tell you something and I wanted to be sure that I had your attention when I said it."

"Okay. You definitely have my attention," I said with a nervous giggle.

"I think you're the most beautiful girl I've ever seen," he confessed wistfully.

I stared at him for a moment. I couldn't tell if he was joking, so I didn't know how to react. The only people that had ever told me before that I was beautiful were Mom, Dad, Stella, and Liam.

"Thanks," I replied suspiciously through narrowed eyes.

"You're welcome," he said with a genuine smile. "Now let's get in there and see what kind of shows are going on today."

With that he opened his door and hopped out. I pulled down the sun blocker and flipped the small lid so I could watch him in the mirror as he opened the trunk and pulled out my wheelchair. He looked so happy that I still couldn't tell if it was a joke. He opened my chair and closed the trunk. I closed the blocker and opened the passenger door.

"How?" he asked with a grin.

I shook my head and smiled, "Out of the way amateur."

Nolan stepped back and I used my hands to grip the roof of the car and pull myself halfway out. I looked over my shoulder at him and my sheepish look told him that I would need help from there.

He slid an arm around my waist and cradled my lower body carefully as he lowered me into the wheelchair. I got comfortable while he locked and closed the doors.

“Ready?” he asked cheerfully.

I looked up at him and nodded. As I put my hands on the wheels, Nolan got behind me and began to push me.

“Um, what are you doing?” I asked in confusion.

“Showing off my hot date,” he replied breezily as he continued to push the chair.

I blushed and laughed. I looked up at him and he gave me his mischievous grin, so I consented and folded my hands in my lap. It would be nice to rest my arms for a day at least.

We got in line to purchase our admissions. The line was moving slowly, so Nolan rested his hands on my shoulders and used his body to roll me forward whenever the line moved.

That's when I noticed a group of teenagers who ranged from at least fifteen to seventeen staring at us. Three boys and three girls looking at us oddly; almost as if trying to figure out what someone like me was doing with someone like Nolan.

I slumped a little in my chair.

"What's wrong, Jane?" Nolan asked.

"Nothing," I replied quietly.

I watched Nolan's shadow as he turned his head to see what had caused my hampered mood.

"You know, Janey, people only stare when they're jealous of what they see. Don't let it bother you," he said loudly.

"Yeah, I wish I had those nasty scars all over my thighs," one of the girls scoffed, causing the others to snicker.

If I had been alone, I would've rolled into her with everything that I had to knock her down. But since I was with Nolan, I couldn't even muster the anger to combat her words. I only felt ashamed for having embarrassed him just by being there.

I put my hands on the wheels and tried to turn around, but Nolan put himself firmly against me and used his foot to stop one of the wheels.

"Any idea what age makes you legally an adult in this state?" he asked me.

I shook my head and blinked back tears, "Why?"

"Because I wonder if I'd go to jail for slapping a child," he replied through clenched teeth.

"You don't have the guts," the girl jeered.

Nolan took an angry step around me but stopped short when we heard our names being called.

“Starr! Nolan!”

I wiped the tears away from my face when I saw Xavier running toward us with a big smile on his face. He had his arms stretched out wide and threw himself against me when he reached us.

“Oh look! She’s got *two* boyfriends!” the girl said as I hugged Xavier. He pulled away instantly.

“She’s not my girlfriend! She’s my friend!” he yelled at her.

“Where are your teeth kid?” one of the boys asked.

“Your mom ate them,” he replied, taking a menacing step forward.

Nolan laughed loudly and even I started to giggle. Xavier looked so fierce that the boy mumbled a “whatever” and put his hands in his pockets.

"Xavier! Leave these nice people alone," a woman who looked just like him said as she approached.

"But Mom, they're my friends!" he protested as she started to drag him away.

"I'm sorry about that," she said to us apologetically.

"It's okay. Hey Xavier, how about a high five buddy?" Nolan asked with a smile.

That's all it took for him to rip away from his mother, come running back, and jump up in the air to high five Nolan.

"Thanks for sticking up for me," I said to him as he walked past me.

"You're welcome!" he said happily as he ran off to join his waiting mother.

Nolan put his hands back on my shoulders and before I knew it, the line had moved so fast that we were at the front. I reached into my pocket for my wallet, but he was faster and paid for our admission.

"I'm buying lunch then," I said.

"No arguments from me," he replied with a grin. "Where do you want to go first?"

I looked at the map in my hand that we had received for free with admission.

"The North Pole? I've always loved Polar Bears."

"Sounds good to me!" he said grabbing the handles and guiding me toward the exhibit. I smiled when I saw the fake icicles and the banner that let us know we had entered the North Pole. In the distance, I heard the Polar Bears muffled roars and I looked up at Nolan with an excited grin.

Of course that grin faded when I saw that standing in front of the actual Polar Bears was that group of teenagers that had just heckled us outside.

"Just ignore them," Nolan said. "And tell me how close you want to get to the exhibit."

"The other end of where they are," I replied quietly.

He chuckled and we went right passed them. He got me as close to the dividing bar as he could and came to stand next to me. I felt the excitement return, when one of the Polar Bears stood on its hind legs to look at everyone that had gathered to see them.

"I remember the last time I saw them. When they did that I was so scared that I hid behind my dad," I said with a laugh.

"And look at you now. All grown up and fearless," Nolan remarked with a smile.

"I wouldn't exactly say fearless. Or grown up," I said smiling back up at him.

The other Polar Bear decided to roll onto its back and yawn. I smiled and nudged Nolan, who smiled down at me in return. My smile slowly disappeared as I looked at him, a random question suddenly on the tip of my tongue.

"Nolan, how old are you?" I asked curiously.

“Younger than that bear, I would imagine” he said nodding at it. I raised an eyebrow in response. “I’m twenty two.”

I nodded.

“Too old to be your friend?” he asked.

“No, I was just curious,” I replied, giving his leg a pat.

Nolan crouched down and turned me to face him.

“Can I ask you something?”

His face was so serious that I automatically nodded.

“I know that we’ve only been hanging out for two days, but -- I really like you. I was wondering if maybe you’d want to be --” he cut his sentence off and looked down for a moment before looking back up at me.

“This is so dumb. I practiced this so much last night that I barely got any sleep and now I can’t say it,” he grumbled.

“Just say it,” I said, putting a hand on his.

"I was wondering if you wanted to be my girlfriend," he mumbled.

I stared at him for a moment. In the twenty years I had been alive so far, no one had ever asked me that before.

"Are you playing a joke on me?" I asked quietly.

"What? No! I really like you and I was just hoping that maybe you liked me too," he said.

"I'd like to be your girlfriend," I said carefully. "But why don't we see how today goes? Then I can answer you for sure."

I watched the half smile spread across his face and he nodded, "Sounds good to me."

I felt shy because he was still crouched in front of me. He still had his hands on either sides of my chair and showed no signs of moving. I looked down at my folded hands, and he used a hand to lift my chin. His eyes wandered to my lips and I felt myself starting to shake a little.

Nolan leaned forward and I took in a sharp breath; he was going to kiss me, I just knew it.

"Once you say yes, I expect a make out session," he whispered in my ear, moving his face away at the last second.

I giggled and he gave me a grin before he stood back up and got behind me.

"Do you like penguins, Janey?" he asked.

"I do!" I replied enthusiastically.

"Then let's venture further into the North Pole. I believe that the penguins are next," he said cheerfully as he guided me into the next room.

"What's your favorite type of penguin?" he asked as I pushed the handicap button on the side of the door.

I thought about it for a moment as the doors opened slowly. "I would have to say The Adelie Penguin, I guess."

"Any particular reason?" he asked, rolling me through the open doors.

"I just think they're so cute. They're the friendlier of the penguins and ... well, once they find their soul mate they stay together for the rest of their lives. I know it sounds weird, but I kind of always wanted to be like them. Social, but still a little awkward and looking for my other penguin half," I said with a sigh.

"I'm pretty sure I can be that penguin. No pressure of course," he said.

I looked up at him and laughed. He didn't meet my gaze, but he grinned nonetheless.

"Hey check that out," he said, suddenly pointing to the left.

I craned my neck to see around the people that were milling about and noticed a small crowd standing around one of the aquarium employees. She was holding something I couldn't quiet see.

"Excuse us," Nolan said rather loudly as he began to maneuver me toward the employee.

He stopped short suddenly. He left me near the back of the crowd and told me that he'd be right back. I watched him curiously as he made his way to the front and started chatting with the employee, before he motioned toward where I was and she followed his gaze. She nodded and started to walk toward me.

I arched my eyebrows at Nolan's mischievous grin.

"Janey, this is Morgan. Morgan this is Jane. Take a look at what she's got," he said to me.

I turned my attention to her and almost squealed. She was holding an Adelie Penguin; an actual Adelie Penguin!

"Is this the one that you like?" Nolan asked.

I nodded enthusiastically as Morgan sat down on the ground in front of me.

"His name is Pogo. He's about two years old and he's quite the character," she said, cradling the animal in her lap.

"Hi, Pogo," I said softly, reaching out a hand. She scooted closer so that I would be able to rub his head. I realized I must've looked like Liam when he got his first baseball glove; goofy, red, and excited, but I was so happy at that moment that I didn't care.

"Do you want to hold him?" she asked me.

I looked up at Nolan who was smiling at me with his hands in his pocket. I looked back at Morgan, then at Pogo.

"If he lets me," I replied hopefully.

"He will. If he didn't like you he would've been crying by now," she said reassuringly.

Morgan pushed herself to her knees and explained to me not to restrain his wings in anyway or he would feel threatened. She also told me that Pogo liked to be best held by letting him stand on your lap and that once he felt comfortable enough, he would lean against you.

I wiped my hands on my shorts before I reached my hands out for Pogo. He slightly opened his little wings while I reached underneath them to put him on my lap. He almost immediately fell against me.

"Wow, I've never seen him do that before," Morgan remarked in surprise. "He must really like you."

I nuzzled the top of his soft head with my cheek. "I really like him too," I said softly.

A flash went off causing me to jump. Pogo shifted in my arms then leaned against me again. I looked up and saw Nolan had his phone out and was taking pictures.

Well, that explains the flash.

"If you want, I take a picture of you and your girlfriend with Pogo," Morgan offered, getting off of the floor.

Nolan looked at me with his half smile and wiggled his eyebrows. I giggled as he handed Morgan his phone and came over to me. He crouched down behind me, put an arm around my shoulder, and pulled me close to him.

"Smile!" she called out as the flash went off again.

She came over to us and gave Nolan his phone back. Then she looked down at me and smiled, "I have to take him back now. Honestly, I wasn't supposed to do that, let you hold him, but I couldn't say no to a girl in a wheelchair. Have a great rest of the guys!"

I let her take Pogo and watched her walk away. My face had become stony. I knew she wasn't being mean, because she had been very kind the whole time, but I felt like I had been pitied.

I hated that feeling.

More than being stuck in this damn wheelchair, I *hated* being pitied.

"What's wrong Janey?" Nolan asked noticing my change in mood.

Of course the wheelchair comment went over his head. He knew Morgan wasn't being mean and he didn't know how much I hated being pitied because I hadn't had the chance to tell him yet.

"Nothing," I mumbled. "Let's go to the dolphin show."

I put my hands on the wheels and began to roll down the wide hallway toward the dolphin exhibit. Nolan caught up to me and grabbed the handles to push me, but I reached back and swatted his hands.

"I can do this myself, you know," I snapped.

"Whoa! What's the matter?" he asked again, stepping around to block my path.

I sighed heavily. I wasn't sure how I was going to explain this to him without sounding like a brat. So I just said what I was feeling.

"I don't want to be treated differently just because I'm in a wheelchair. If she shouldn't have done it then she shouldn't have done it. Giving me special treatment because of this damn chair makes me feel pitied and I hate that feeling."

"She didn't mean any harm by it, but I get what you're saying. My thoughts are this; don't let anyone's words get too close to your heart. Whether they hurt your or make you feel good. They all start out disguised as lies and you only ever see their true intentions in your weakest moment. Know what I mean?" he said.

That was the deepest thing that Nolan had said to me so far. Not to mention one of the most intelligent statements I had ever heard. I completely saw his point; words were deceptive. Good or bad, *all* forms of words were deceptive.

"I guess," I conceded with a shrug. Then another random question materialized in my mind. "Nolan, why don't you call me Starr anymore?"

"I like Jane. I kind of feel like it's more personal. I hope you don't mind."

"I'm sorry I got so angry," I said quietly.

"Don't apologize. It's always refreshing to see different human emotions," he said falling into step beside me, as I began to wheel myself toward the dolphins.

"You're kind of really smart," I observed.

Nolan laughed held open one of the doors for me. I smiled at him as I rolled into the auditorium. I found a spot in the back that was designated the handicap spot and I waited for Nolan to go around me before I folded my hands in my lap. He leaned over and took one of my hands in his as more people filled the auditorium.

I sat there happily as the trainers ran out. But it wasn't that I was going to see one of the best shows I'd ever seen that made me happy. It was that Nolan was holding my hand so tightly in his.

My thoughts were drowned out by the roar from the crowd as the dolphins suddenly appeared in the pool beneath us. I cheered along with them which made Nolan laugh. I looked over at him with excited eyes and he grinned.

Then his grin faded as he looked behind me.

Suddenly my chair was lurched forward and I was launched toward the stairs. My hands went out wildly as I tried to grab onto something, anything that would stop my destructive descent down the concrete stairs.

"Janey! Someone help her!" Nolan yelled as he ran down the steps behind me.

Immediately the crowd sprang to life as people ran out into the aisle to try to stop me and always missing by two seconds. I saw the balcony coming closer as I bumped viciously down the stairs.

This is going to hurt so much, I thought fearfully as someone managed to stop the wheelchair.

I fell out of it and rolled down the remainder of the stairs, my body hitting the concrete balcony divider. Something, somewhere inside of me snapped and I felt a rush of exquisite pain wash over me.

I landed on my stomach thankfully. I was so embarrassed that I didn't want to have to face anyone. I felt someone's hands on my arm and I could faintly hearing them ask me if I was okay.

"Don't move her! Wait for the paramedics!" the same voice said forcefully.

"Is she okay? Janey? Can you hear me?" Nolan sounded so frantic that if I wasn't already in so much pain, I probably would have shed a tear.

I put my hands underneath myself and attempted to push myself up but the first voice stopped me.

"Honey, don't. You could be seriously injured and moving without the paramedics here can, and will only make it worse. They've been paged and should be here soon."

Then I felt something big and frabricy being draped across my back. It was a jacket and it belonged to a man; I could tell by the smell of cologne and cigarettes.

"I need you to calm down, son. You look like you're about to crawl out of your skin. She's going to be fine," the man said to Nolan.

I felt a burning sensation starting in my leg where I had the unsuccessful surgery to replace my rotten femur bone. One of many unsuccessful surgeries that lead to the Freddy Krueger claw inspired scars I had on my thighs.

"Excuse us please!" a new voice said forcefully.

"They're here now, honey. You're going to be okay," the man said.

I felt his jacket pulled off of me by the paramedics. I felt a board that they placed next to my arm and leg, before they gently rolled me onto it.

"Does your neck hurt?" the female asked me.

"No," I whispered.

“I’d feel better if you had a neck brace on. Is that okay?” she asked, pulling it out and securing it around me before I had a chance to respond.

I closed my eyes tightly for a moment, trying to push the pain out of my mind. When I opened them again, I cut my eyes in all directions trying to find Nolan.

I finally found him standing behind one of the EMT’s and his face was heartbreaking; red, tear stained, angry, and scared.

“Any idea what happened here?” the male paramedic asked him as they began to climb the stairs with me.

“She was – the chair, it rolled,” he said.

The paramedic eyed him suspiciously as they reached the top ground with me. They hoisted me onto a stretcher and began to walk out of the aquarium with me.

They took me outside, loaded me into the ambulance, and the female came in the back with me.

"Where are you taking her?" Nolan asked.

"Redwood Medical," she said. "Call her parents and have them meet us there."

"No!" I managed to yell. I closed my eyes as the pain pulsed through me sharper than before at my sudden outburst.

"Honey, we need consent to treat you," she said.

"I'm twenty years old. I can consent. Nolan?" I called out weakly.

"I'm here Janey," he said leaning into the ambulance.

"Don't call them. Just be there when I get there, okay?"

"I promise."

The doors to the ambulance were slammed shut and the sirens started up.

That was the last thing I remembered about my day at the aquarium with Nolan.

Five

I guess it was about a week and a half later when I was woken by the sound of pacing in my room. My eyes fluttered a little and I heard Liam yelling that I was awake.

I put a hand to my head for a moment before I fully opened my eyes. I saw Stella's face hovering a few inches from mine. I smiled at her and she fell against me giving me the biggest hug she could muster.

"I was scared, Starr," she said tearfully. "You were asleep for a really long time."

"I'm fine, Rabbit. I guess I was just sleepy," I replied, rubbing her back reassuringly.

"Jane?"

I looked over at my mother who was sitting next to the bed nervously wringing her hands. Behind her I saw my father and deduced that it was him that had to be pacing.

"Hi guys," I said weakly as Liam climbed onto the bed and hugged me as tightly as Stella did.

Mom, Dad, Rabbit, and Nugget. Where's Nolan? I wondered looking around.

"Aaron, why don't you take the kids down to the cafeteria so I can talk to Jane," she said glancing up at him.

He grunted and plucked the children off of the bed. Dad hovered over me for a moment with tears in his eyes before he leaned down and kissed my forehead. I smiled at him and he left the room with Stella and Liam.

"I'm so happy you're awake, sweetheart," she said softly.

"Me too. I guess I just needed a good night's sleep."

"Jane, you been asleep for a week," she replied seriously.

"A ... week?"

How is that possible?

"I need you to tell me exactly what happened and why you were so far away from home."

"He just wanted to do something nice, so that's where he decided to take me. And I don't know what happened Mom. One minute I was sitting next to him holding his hand and the next I was flying down the stairs," I replied truthfully.

"Yeah that sounds like what he told us," she replied thoughtfully.

"Where is he anyway? He promised he'd be here when I got here."

"He was Janey. The hospital called us to let us know that you were here and what happened. He was in the waiting room practically beside himself with guilt. Aaron ... You know how your father can be," she finished heavily.

"Daddy made him leave, didn't he?" I asked sadly.

"Yes. He also told him that he's not allowed to come anywhere near you again. That his carelessness with you is what put you in danger for the second time," she said quietly.

"That's not fair! He was just trying to be a good friend!"

That's all it took for me to burst into uncontrollable sobs. Two simple sentences.

"Honey, whether he meant to or not, he put you in danger. Especially by not telling us where he was really taking you," Mom said brushing my hair out of my face.

I couldn't even respond. The one friend I had made, the *one* person that truly made me feel good about myself, was officially banned from my life.

"Jane, would it help if I told you that he's been coming by the hospital every night? Not inside, but I've been meeting him out in the parking garage to let him know how you're doing. That way he doesn't have to run into Aaron and ... and ... he knows that you're still with us."

I took a deep breath to try to stop the tears, but it was no use. I was too far gone into critical life crisis mode that I wasn't going to recover from this any time soon.

"I know what you need," she said. Mom got up from her chair and went to the door. She peeked her head out before coming back to my side and grabbing the telephone receiver from the table next to her. I heard her punch in some numbers. After a brief conversation, she handed the phone to me. I was doing the wrecked breathing motions that come with coming down from the earth shattering sobs, so I hadn't heard who she was speaking to or realized that the phone was being handed to me.

"Jane, take this phone and hurry before Aaron comes back," she said urgently, pushing the receiver next to my ear.

I turned my head slightly and sniffled into the receiver. Mom placed it between my shoulder and my ear. She had the phone on her lap so that I wouldn't have to adjust myself too much.

"Hey Janey," a voice said softly.

I immediately started to cry again. In between gasps for air and fresh tears, I managed to gasp out a few "I'm sorries". While I was of the mind that my father should have been the one on the phone right now apologizing to Nolan, I knew he was too stubborn to ever do so.

"I can barely understand you," he said with a chuckle.

"Mom ... told ... me that ... you ... were here," I gasped between sobs.

"Well, I promised, didn't I?"

I took a few more shuddery breaths. I wanted to be able to speak to him and if I kept crying, Dad would walk in and catch me.

"Can you come visit me please?" I asked in a small voice.

"Oh Janey," he said sadly. "I want to more than you know, but Mr. East ..."

I must've looked completely shattered, because Mom reached over and grabbed the phone from me.

"Nolan, you come by tomorrow morning and you stay here all day with Jane. I'll figure out what do with Aaron and the kids," she said, before hanging up.

"How are you going to manage that?" I asked her.

"I'll figure it out. I want you to understand that I'm very upset with Nolan for not telling us where you would be and for not calling us when you had your accident. But ... he seems to make you happy. So I'll do my best to make sure you have the day together tomorrow. Even if I have to slash all the tires on the cars," she said with a look of determination on her face.

Stella's voice rang down the hallway and Mom put the phone back where it had originally sat. Dad reentered the room with them and Liam came over to me with a small cup of vanilla ice cream.

"I made this for you, Starr. And Stella helped!" he said proudly, holding it out to me.

"The staff told them they couldn't take it out of the cafeteria, but they insisted," Dad said shaking his head.

"Thanks guys, I'll eat it in a little bit," I replied with a big smile.

Mom suddenly got up from her seat and left. Dad sat down in her chair with a heavy sigh and looked at me.

"How are you feeling, kiddo?" he asked softly.

"I'm fine Daddy. I just can't believe I slept that long is all," I lied.

"I'm glad you're okay," he said clearing his throat. I glanced over at him and he turned his face. Dad was crying and he didn't want me to see.

"I'll *always* be okay, Daddy," I replied. "I just need you to start trusting me."

"I do trust *you*," he said meaningfully.

I sighed as Mom walked back in. She told my father that since I was awake now and everything seemed to be okay (she had just come from talking to the doctor) that it would be best if they let me rest for the rest of today and tomorrow. He grudgingly agreed and the children climbed on the bed to hug me again. Dad leaned over and kissed my forehead. Mom hugged me and slid a piece of paper under my arm.

"We love you, honey," she said. "We'll see you in a couple of days, okay?"

I nodded and waited for them to walk out before I checked the note. It was a phone number and small note from Mom all at the same time.

Call this number was soon as we walk out. It's all taken care of for you, Mom.

I reached for the phone and set it next to me on the bed. Curiously, I dialed the number.

"Hello?"

It was Nolan.

"Hi," I said softly.

"I'm on my way. Your mother called me after she arranged everything with the nurses and doctor. I'll see you soon Janey."

He hung up with no further explanation of what Mom had done. I sighed and put the phone back. I closed my eyes for a moment and let my breathing steady itself. It would take him at least forty five minutes to get here so a short nap wouldn't be out of order.

But I opened my eyes again, after I reasoned with myself that I had already slept for a week, and that would be ungodly redundant. I looked out the window and watched the cars going by on the freeway. I watched the birds flying high above the cars. And I watched the clouds starting to fuse together for perhaps a quick rain storm.

I heard one of the nurses come into the room to check my IV and I heard her walk out as the rain drops started to slowly pelt the window. I heard the hospital personnel walking in the hallways and I heard the sounds of carts being wheeled by. Or people; I wasn't sure which.

More rain drops fell against the window and I smiled. I loved when it rained; it was such a calming thing to watch and the way the world smelled after was such a delight.

The storm moved in quickly as the sky darkened to a stone gray. A flash of lighting lit up the sky and was immediately followed by a clap of thunder. The window became a blurry, wet view but I didn't turn away from it.

"What are we looking at?" a voice whispered next to my ear.

I jumped so hard, that the bed shook. I turned my face toward the voice and started to laugh. Nolan looked as startled as I felt.

"Geez, Janey. I didn't realize how jumpy you were," he said shaking his head.

"Well, you *did* just scare the shit out of me," I replied.

He smiled the genuine light-up-my-world smile. I smiled back before turning my attention back to the blurry world outside.

"You know I kind of want to sit down, but I'd be obstructing your view if I did," Nolan said with a laugh.

"Actually, you should sit. I'd bet you look amazing with a thunderstorm backdrop," I said matter-of-factly.

"Are you flirting with me Janey?" he asked with a grin as he settled into the chair in front of me.

I rolled my eyes but couldn't fight the smile forming on my face. Nolan leaned onto the bed and looked at me for a moment before speaking.

"I have been worried sick about you. Jessie's been great with keeping me in the loop of how you've been. I think she realized how much I cared about you when Mr. East kicked me out of here and I destroyed half of the waiting room on the way out," he said with a chuckle.

"That's so weird," I remarked.

"I just didn't want to leave you," he replied with a shrug.

"No, not that. The fact that you called Mom Jessie, and Dad Mr. East."

"I don't think he'd appreciate me referring to him as, Aaron," he replied dryly. "I'm not his favorite person at the moment."

"It wasn't your fault though," I said, reaching up and brushing his hair behind his ear.

Another flash of lighting. A booming clap of thunder. Nolan really did look beautiful with the storm raging behind him. It made his emerald eyes look more precious for some reason.

"I never answered your question, by the way," I said letting my hand rest on his.

"Oh, I haven't forgotten," he replied wiggling his eyebrows and grinning.

I smiled and let my eyes wander to the window for a moment.

"You know, I didn't tell my parents this, but when I landed I heard something snap. Inside of me. Do you know if the doctor ever found out what it was?" I asked.

"I can go ask," he offered.

"They won't tell you," I replied shaking my head. "You're not immediate family. Hold on; let me buzz the nurse."

A moment later, a nurse materialized.

"Hello Jane. It's good to see you awake," she said with a pleasant smile.

She was older with a smattering of gray hair, a kind face, and crow's feet. She was unreasonably thin and was swimming in her scrubs. But I honestly liked her right away.

“My name is Debbie and I’m your nurse,” she continued.

“Hi Debbie. This is Nolan,” I said, gesturing toward him.

“Hello young man,” she said warmly.

He blushed and smiled in return.

“So, what can I do for you Jane?” she asked turning her attention back to me.

“When I fell, I heard something snap. Did you do any X-Rays on me, by some chance?” I asked curiously.

“We did.”

Silence.

“And did you find anything?” I asked.

“Yes.”

Silence.

“Can you tell me what you found?”

Her eyes traveled to Nolan for a moment, before she shook her head.

"Oh if it's because he's here, it's okay. He's cool," I said breezily.

"It's not so much that. It's just ... Well I remember the first night he was here. It's obvious that he cares a great deal about you," she explained uneasily.

Then it's not good news. Great.

"Nolan, do you want to know? Or do you want to wait outside?" I asked him.

"I would rather know, then not," he replied quietly.

Debbie sat down on the side of the bed and took my hand.

"When you had your accident, you cracked your femur bone wide open. We think it caused an infection because you spiked a fever when you passed out. We're going to be keeping you here for a little while. Just to be on the safe side," she said.

"No wonder I was in so much pain," I said more to myself than her.

"Is she going to be okay?" Nolan asked.

"We don't know dear. That's why we're keeping her here."

What?

"Um, I feel fine actually. If I had an infection, wouldn't I be boiling still?" I asked.

"While that may be true, we have to we'll have to perform another surgery on your femur, Jane," she said softly.

"No."

"Jane, you don't understand; if we don't and the infection spreads --"

"No thank you," I insisted cutting her off.

"Janey --"

"Please don't, Nolan. I don't want any more surgeries."

Debbie looked at me for a moment before she stood up and walked out.

"Jane, you have to do this. Please. I won't be able to live with myself if ... if something happens to you because I took you to the aquarium," he said, his voice breaking.

"Nolan I'll be fine. I promise. I've had worse things than an infection happen to me since I've wound up with wheels," I said to him.

"Promise?"

"Promise."

Six

Two weeks later I was able to go home. Just in time for my twenty first birthday which was the next day. I hadn't seen Nolan since because my father refused to leave me again after that. He was especially upset that I signed off on a medical piece of paper saying that I was refusing the surgery.

I spent most of the day laying in my bed, with Rabbit and Nugget curled up on either side of me. We were watching *Cartoon Network* and it was the greatest feeling in the world.

They were well behaved until the sun went down and Mom came in to tell them that they would have to go upstairs and get in bed. They both protested saying that they hadn't watched TV with me in so long. Mom didn't budge and told them that I needed my rest.

When everyone was gone, I settled in and flipped through the channels. I settled on *Gone*

With The Wind and after an hour slipped into a half sleep, half conscious state.

I was awoken by the tapping at my window. I opened my eyes and rolled over onto my back and smiled. It was Nolan and he was motioning for me to open the window. I held up a hand so that he would stop tapping. He nodded and I reached for my chair. I first went to my bedroom door and locked it so no one could walk in then I rolled over to the window and unlocked it, pushing it up enough for him to stick his hands underneath and push it the rest of the way open.

"Hi," he said softly as he climbed in.

"Hi," I replied.

He glanced at the TV and smiled.

"Great movie," he remarked.

"I've never seen it," I admitted.

"Shame. One day you'll have to watch it from the beginning."

"Maybe. So, what's up?" I asked quietly.

"I missed you," he said.

I looked up at him. He was still staring at the TV and I felt that fluttering feeling again.

“I missed you too,” I responded truthfully.

He finally tore his eyes away from the movie and smiled at me. He sat on the edge of the bed and pulled me close to him.

“So. How about an answer to that question?” he asked softly.

“Ask me again.”

“Will you be my girlfriend?”

“Yes,” I replied without hesitation.

He smiled and took my face into his hands. Instead of pulling me toward him, he leaned forward and gently pressed his lips against mine.

My first real kiss.

And it was perfect.

It was with someone that I genuinely liked and it was the day before my birthday; not many other gifts would be able to compare to this.

When Nolan pulled back, I was shaking and so was he. I could feel it and it made me shy for some reason.

"Was it okay to do that?" he asked.

I nodded and he smiled.

"Can you help me get back into the bed?" I asked him.

Nolan got up from the bed and cradled me in his arms. (One of the places I found to be the safest in the world.) He pushed my chair against the door and as I got comfortable in the bed, he pulled his shoes and jacket off and climbed into bed with me.

I turned slightly and looked at him with wide eyes.

"Don't worry, Janey. I just want to lay here with you," he whispered.

I nodded and turned my eyes back to *Gone With The Wind,* but when Nolan cuddled up against me and wrapped an arm around my waist, I almost immediately fell asleep. He emanated so much body heat, that I felt like I was sleeping next to a heater. Not that I minded. I just wished I was able to keep my eyes open so that I could remember how it felt to have him this close to me.

It was a strange thought to have and I didn't know where it came from. Nonetheless, I fell asleep within ten minutes of having Nolan's arm around me.

I woke up the next morning to someone knocking on my door.

"Starr? Are you awake?"

It was Dad.

I rolled over and began jostling Nolan. He had to wake up and get out.

Now.

"What the hell?" he asked, sitting up.

"Dad's knocking at the door. You have to go," I whispered urgently.

He sprang from the bed and grabbed his jacket. I watched him slide his shoes on and head to the window. He opened it quietly and was half way out when he climbed back in.

"Starr?" Dad asked, again pounding louder.

"You have to go!" I whispered frantically as my father began to fiddle with the doorknob.

Nolan came back over to the bed and looked at me with his half smile.

"Kiss me and I'll leave."

I stared at him for a moment and considered letting my father in. Only because I shouldn't have to be backed into a corner to kiss him. But I saw his dimples starting to deepen in his face and his eyes seemed to sparkle.

"Okay," I replied with a grin.

Nolan leaned down and put his hands on either side of me and kissed me. In fact, he kissed me so breathtakingly, that I fell back against the bed and pulled him toward me.

"Jane Camille East! You open this door this minute!" Dad yelled. He probably heard the footsteps and the bed creaking, I reasoned.

"*Camille*?" Nolan asked quietly after he pulled away.

"Yeah, I know. Now go before he breaks the door down," I whispered.

"I'll come back tonight when everyone's asleep. Happy Birthday, Janey," he said, kissing me one more time, before he made his way to the window.

Dad managed to push the door open as soon as Nolan disappeared. One second sooner and he would have caught him.

"Why was your door blocked?" he asked me suspiciously.

"I was up watching TV late. I probably didn't secure the chair," I shrugged.

He glanced around the room and then back at me.

"I thought I heard footsteps," he said, putting his hands on his hips.

“You probably just heard that,” I said pointing at the TV. Thankfully, I had left it on when I fell asleep with Nolan.

“Well, it’s your birthday, Janey,” he said, his voice softening.

I smiled.

Daddy was probably sad because I wasn’t going to go out and do “normal” twenty one year old things. Like walk into a bar and get so drunk that I would have to be dragged out by all of the friends I didn’t have.

“It’s going to be a great day,” I said cheerfully. I shoved off my sheets and Dad came over to help me get into my chair.

“What do you want to do today?” he asked.

“I don’t know,” I said thoughtfully. “Maybe we can find a way to get me upstairs? I wouldn’t mind just sitting around with Stella and Liam in their room.”

“Anything else?” he asked with a smile.

“Well.”

Here goes nothing.

"I'm sure that Nolan would like to come over."

"No."

"But Daddy --"

"Janey," Dad said letting out a long suffering sigh. "I don't want that boy anywhere near you. It's not because I don't like him; I do. But he lied to us, me and your mother, about where he was taking you. That could have cost you your life if the hospital hadn't called us. You were unconscious and you weren't able to consent to treatment."

"Please? It's the only thing I really want," I said close to tears.

Dad sighed again and walked away. He left me looking after him somewhere between my bedroom and the bathroom.

I stayed there for a moment. I heard him in the living room whispering furiously with Mom. I sighed and rolled into the bathroom to start my morning routine. Ten minutes later when I emerged, my parents were waiting for me in the hallway.

"Your father told me what you would like for your birthday. After some discussion," she said glancing at my father, "we've decided to invite Nolan over. There are some stipulations though."

I was so happy that I agreed to everything they said.

The stipulations were as followed:

1. I would have one hour with Nolan in Stella and Liam's room. The door was to remain open.

2. I would have one additional hour alone with Nolan in my room; with the door open.

3. I would agree to not see Nolan without my parent's permission and without full disclosure of where would be going.

"Thank you!" I said when she was done. I was beyond ecstatic. I reached over for both of my parents and they both hugged me tightly.

Once we broke apart, I rolled into the kitchen to call Nolan and give him the good news.

Seven

Nolan arrived a half an hour later. I tried to beat Dad to the door, but since he could walk and I couldn't, he made it there first. I was in the living room with Mom and I craned my head to get a glimpse of Nolan.

He looked borderline terrified, borderline apprehensive.

"Hello Nolan," my father said sternly. It was more of a growl than a greeting.

"Mr. East."

"You have two hours. I trust that Starr gave you the rules," he said.

"Yes, sir. Thank you for having me over," he replied stiffly.

Dad nodded and finally stepped back to let him in. Mom rushed forward and gave Nolan a big hug.

I smiled. Things were so backwards lately. Usually it was Dad saving the day after Mom made something uncomfortable. When she pulled away I locked eyes with Nolan and he smiled. (The genuine happy-to-see-you smile.)

"Come on, Aaron," my mother said, as she went over to my father and gently grabbed him by the arm. It took a few tugs before he relented and let her walk him out of the room.

"Oh, hey. Mr. East?" Nolan called out.

Dad spun around immediately and looked at him questioningly.

"Does my hour start now or when you opened the door?"

I had to stifle a giggle. While it was a truly valid question, I could hear the slight sarcasm in his tone.

"Your hour starts when the two of you are in the kids' room or alone in Starr's," Mom answered.

"Thanks Mrs. E," he replied with a nod.

She smiled and yanked Dad out of the room. Nolan came over and kissed me quickly before sitting down next to me on the couch.

"So, my parents want to meet you," he said conversationally.

"Why?" I asked more defensively than I meant to.

"Morbid curiosity I would imagine," he replied with a shrug.

"Ah, the 'why is my son in love with a girl in a wheelchair' morbidity," I said knowingly.

"Actually it's more 'We can't believe he's in love, we have to meet the girl who's the object of his affection' curiosity," he amended.

"And would you say that you're in love?" I asked tilting my head.

"I could be convinced to share my feelings of intimacy with you," he said clearing his throat.

"Oh?"

"Yes, but ... There's something I would require from you first."

"What's that?"

He shifted on the chair so that I could see how serious he had suddenly become.

"I need you to promise that you'll only reply truthfully. I don't want to be told what I want to hear when I make this disclosure. I want to hear what you truly and honestly feel."

"Fair enough."

"The first time your parents came to my house to welcome us to the neighborhood, I could see how tired they looked. Not physically, but emotionally. I've always been empathetic I guess and I could tell that something was weighing heavily on them. Now, mind you, I was in a different room hiding behind a door watching them talk to my parents, before I was called in and formally introduced. They shared a glance and asked me how old I was. I told them and that's when they asked me if I would like to come over and meet you. Possibly try to get you out of the house more often; on a strictly friendly basis only. I agreed when they told me how you were ... chair bound. I guess it reminded me of when I was on crutches and no one wanted to play with me," he said with a chuckle.

"So this was a pity friendship?" I asked.

"Not at all, Janey. Let me finish please. Anyway, did you know that your father carries a shit ton of pictures of you in his wallet? Like, I mean when he opened it, a foldout hit the floor. He has everything in there from when you were born to a few months ago when Stella turned seven. My parents thought it was a little weird, I thought it was great. I remember that Dad asked him why he carried so many pictures. Probably thinking you were terminal and your father told him it was because he loved you so much and wished you had a normal life. Your mother started sniffling while I went through the pictures. Mom asked her to join her in the kitchen. I knew it was so she could cry and I pretended not to notice. Back to the pictures though. There was one of you holding Liam when he was just born. You were smiling so grandly and Stella was standing next to your chair making a face. You had an arm around her and were struggling to hold Liam. But I think it's the way you held your little brother. The way you made sure Stella still felt wanted, so loving and awkward at the same time ... That's around the time that I truly and helplessly fell in love with you," he finished glancing at me.

I opened my mouth but nothing came out, so I closed it. I took a deep breath and opened my mouth again but only a squeak came out.

I wasn't trying to be coy and I wasn't trying to be cute. I was honestly at a loss for words. I hadn't expected a speech. I only expected a yes or no.

"So, I have to ask this now. Do *you* love *me*?" Nolan inquired.

"What I have to say will not be as meaningful as what just presented, so please don't hate me. All I can honestly say is that what I feel for you is much more than I ever thought I could feel for anyone. I've never been in love before, but I would imagine that this would be it."

He let out a huge sigh and sat back against the couch. I watched him, wanting to reach over and kiss him, when the kids came barreling into the room.

"Nolan!" they both yelled happily, jumping on him.

"Hey guys!" he said enthusiastically.

"It's Starr's birthday!" Liam told him.

"That's right! Did you bring her a present?" Stella asked, pulling away from him.

"He already gave it to me," I answered with a smile.

"What'd you get?" she asked excitedly coming over to me.

"A very special promise," Nolan said mysteriously.

"You can't wear a promise," Stella said in disappointment.

"Rabbit, not every present has to be something material. What Nolan just promised me is something no one else ever has," I said reprimanded.

She pouted for a moment, before her seven year old mind took over, and she told us to go upstairs with her and Liam.

When we got to the stairs, Nolan leaned down. I lifted my arms, expecting him to cradle me, but instead he stood me on my feet. A sharp pain shot through my left leg and I winced.

"Today Janey, on your twenty first birthday, you're going to fulfill a dream. You're going to *walk* up to kids' rooms," he said getting behind me.

I felt tears welling in my eyes and I didn't know if it was because he had so much faith in me or if it was because the pain kept resonating throughout my body.

"I don't think I can," I said miserably.

"Yes you can, Starr!" Liam said. I looked up and saw him and Stella sitting at the top of the stairs waiting for me. They both had huge, encouraging smiles on their faces.

"I won't let you fall. Promise," Nolan whispered into my ear.

I looked down at my feet and up at the long arduous task in front of me. I took a deep breath and put my hand on the railing. Nolan put his hands on my hips to steady me and I bent my leg.

My first footstep turned out to be quite agonizing. And it wasn't the fact that I bent my leg or that I moved my hips; it was putting my foot down and putting pressure on it that made me bite my lip and blink back tears.

"Hold on," Nolan said. I think he noticed the problem as quickly as I felt it. He used his hand to gently move my foot off of the step. He shifted again behind me and gently raised me high enough to place my feet on top of his. With an arm around my waist, he slowly began to climb up the stairs, careful not to step too harshly on the steps.

Now I get it; I didn't exactly walk up the stairs by myself. But Nolan did his best and something no one had ever thought to do before him. Since my legs and hips couldn't take the weight of me on top of them, he gave me the *sensation* of walking, by letting me use his feet to rest my weight on.

"Mommy! Daddy! Come see! Starr's walking!" Liam yelled proudly at the top of his lungs.

"Liam, what in the world are you yelling about? Mom asked entering the room. "And where is your big sister?"

I took my hand off of the banister and raised it.

"Oh my God, Aaron! AARON COME QUICK!" Mom yelled half crying half laughing.

"Jessie, what are you the children screaming about?" Dad asked in exasperation.

Nolan took the last step up the stairs and onto the second floor landing. He hugged me tightly against him and I smiled at the kids. They were whooping and jumping up and down.

"Turn me around," I said to him.

Slowly, he turned making sure to keep my feet on his and to balance both of us.

"Hi Daddy," I said waving.

He put a hand to his mouth and even from where I stood I could see the tears starting to spill over onto his cheeks.

"I walked up the stairs. Are you proud of me?" I asked, gripping Nolan's arms.

"I've never been so proud of you in my life," he said through his tears.

"Taking her back down the stairs will be easier and lot faster. And just as safe, I assure you," Nolan said to my parents.

Dad nodded and reached for my chair. He folded it and began to climb the stairs when Nolan shook his head.

"Unnecessary Mr. East. We'll be walking today for as long as our legs can hold us," he said, giving me a gentle squeeze. He turned us around and smiled at the kids. "Let's go!"

"Come on guys! Let's go play!" Stella said, happily leading the way to her and Liam's room.

Eight

It took ten minutes for me to get properly adjusted on the floor. Stella said that I could sit with my back leaning against the end of her bed and Liam brought me his coloring table to use. Nolan had carefully straightened my legs out in front of me and then we all chose a box of crayons and some construction paper. Multi-colored of course.

At the suggestion of Liam, everyone made me a birthday card. I laughed when he said it because he looked so excited about it. So while they all busied themselves with coloring pictures on the front of the card and writing things inside, I busied myself with making thank you cards for each of them.

When we were all done, Stella insisted that everyone stand up and read their card to me before letting me have them. She also insisted that she go first.

"Dear Janey, Thank you for being born. You are the best big sister anyone could ever ask for. I love you very much and wish we had a party for you. Love, Stella."

She handed me the card and gave me a big hug. I thanked her and gave her the thank you card I had made for her and she grinned widely.

As she went and sat back down, Liam stood up.

"Dear Janey, I wish that I could give you my legs as a birthday present so that you wouldn't have to be in that wheelchair. But I can't. I'm sorry. I love you, Liam."

"Oh Nugget," I whispered tearfully when he hugged me. I took the card from him and gave him his thank you card.

Nolan stood up and cleared his throat nervously.

"Jane, I've never in my life met anyone that I believe in as much as I do you. I believe in the fact that you are the kindest person I've ever met. I believe in the fact that your love is so strong for others and that your heart is so big, that you have to be confined. I believe it wouldn't be fair to the world to have someone as beautiful and endearing as you to be able to walk too, so you were given an obstacle. But in the little bit of time that I've known you, I've realized it isn't an obstacle at all. That while there are times that you seem unhappy because of your situation, you rarely let it show on the outside. That is why I wanted to ask you a very important question." He looked up at me for a moment, then back down to his birthday card. "Will you, Jane Camille East, do me the honor of marrying me?"

"Yes!" the kids yelled together.

I was crying by that point. I wanted to say yes, more than anything in the world, but I also knew that if I did I would become a burden on someone new. I didn't want him to have to take care of me for the rest of my life. I loved Nolan more than I could put into words, but ... I couldn't do that to him.

"I can't," I sobbed.

"Yes you can."

I looked up and saw Mom and Dad had been standing in the doorway. I didn't know how long they had been there, but their faces were red and they looked like they were both fighting back tears.

"You deserve to be happy too. Even though I think this entire *friendship* moved way too quickly toward this, you can't help what your heart wants. And Nolan's heart wants you, Janey," my father said.

I held up my hands and took a deep breath. I needed to steady myself for what I was going to tell them. After about five minutes of hiccup breathing, I was finally able to talk.

"I can't be a burden to everyone that loves me. And that's what I'll be to you," I said looking up at Nolan. "I can't take a bath or a shower without Mom undressing me and putting me in the bath chair. I can't find anywhere that will hire me, so I wouldn't be able to pull in half of what we would need to support ourselves. We'd need to build a special kitchen where I could reach everything just to be able to cook for you. We'd need ramps installed so I can get in and out of the house when you aren't home. I wouldn't be able to give you children; that's something that everyone deserves."

Nolan came over to where I was sitting and knelt down beside me. He took my hands in his and put his forehead against mine.

"Everything you just said is either material or trivial. True love doesn't ask for anything other than the person it wants. I'd be happy living in the streets if you were with me. I don't need a big fancy house; I don't need children, hell I don't even need you to cook for me. I.Just.Need.You."

Fresh tears poured of my eyes and Nolan kissed me gently. He took a deep breath and let it out after a moment.

"Jane. I think he deserves an answer. One from your heart and not your mind," Daddy said.

"Are you sure you want a life like this?" I asked gesturing around me.

"Positive."

I took a deep breath and looked at Stella and Liam who were watching us with big hopeful eyes. I looked over at my mom as she leaned her head onto my dad's shoulder. I watched him put his arm around her and hold her close to him. I looked down for a moment and then back up into Nolan's expectant face.

"Then yes. I will marry you," I whispered.

As he leaned in and kissed me, hard and passionately, my father cleared his throat.

"Considering that she's only twenty one and you're twenty two, I expect a long engagement. Furthermore --"

"Oh honestly Aaron! Let them have this moment before you start filling it with demands," my mother said, dragging him away from the door.

"Stella! Liam! Come here please!" Mom called over her shoulder.

"Does this mean you're going to be our brother?" Liam whispered as he walked past us.

"Yeah, I guess it does," Nolan answered.

Liam hugged him tightly before he ran out of the room.

"So ..." Nolan said.

"So ..."

"I was kind of wondering if you really said yes or if this is a dream," he said with a laugh.

"I did indeed say yes," I assured him.

He sat next to me and I put my head on his shoulder. "I feel like this isn't official until I present you with a ring of engagement. Fortunately, I have one in mind. I'll bring it to you tonight."

"I would think that as my fiancée you should be able to just walk in the front door," I reasoned.

"A'scuse me," Liam said, poking his head into the room. "Daddy wants to talk to both of you."

I sighed heavily. I had a feeling that our special moment wasn't going to last very long. Nolan got to his feet, bringing me up with him. I hovered in his arms as he slid his feet underneath mine and walked me toward the door. When we reached the top of the stairs, he sat down and secured me on his lap.

"Ready?" he asked mischievously.

"For what?" I asked in confusion.

"To go down, of course."

He used his hands to give us a start down the stairs, before securing his arms rightly around me. I closed my eyes and let out a little squeal of terror and joy as we rode down the staircase on his rear end.

I laughed when we got to the bottom. Nolan was laughing too and Mom looked amused. Dad on the other hand, opened my wheelchair and scooped me off of Nolan.

"I need you to start being a little more responsible," he said quietly to me as he lowered me onto the chair.

"Yes Dad. Sorry about that."

Nolan was sitting on the third from bottom step, his hands locked in front of him, as he waited for Dad to talk to both of us.

"I just wanted to say a couple of things," he finally said clearing his throat. "I am aware that when you get married, you'll want to move out and have a home of your own. I don't expect that day to be a long time from now. (Mom sighed heavily and rolled her eyes.) But what I do expect is for Jane to stay here with us until you've found a place for the two of you to live. We know best how her daily routine goes and we need you to become aware and accustomed to it before you can take her."

I exchanged a glance with Nolan. I saw his half smile starting to sneak across his face and I wondered if any smart ass remark would come out of him.

"Mr. East, I understand what you're saying. And while I would like to take her off of your hands right now, just push her straight out the door and never look back, I completely concede that it wouldn't be responsible. On any level. So, if I may, I'd like to counter your offer."

I raised an eyebrow at him, but he was careful not to look at me.

"Go on," Dad said crossing his arms over his chest.

"As her betrothed, I think that you should let her move in with me and my parents, or let me move in here. We're not going to do anything under your roof that would be disrespectful, but if you want me to learn her daily routine, the easiest way would be is for me to observe from when she wakes up until she goes to sleep. Wouldn't you agree?"

My eyes became huge. Nolan still wouldn't look at me. He was intent on holding my father's gaze. I looked at my mother who looked as equally surprised and horrified as I did.

Now I wasn't horrified at the prospect of living with Nolan under anyone's roof. I mean, his argument made sense. To learn, he'd have to observe from beginning to end. No, what worried me was how my father, Aaron East, was going to react.

"Call your parents and ask them to come over please," he said curtly as he walked out of the hallway.

Mom looked as confused as I felt. I expected him to put his foot down and completely deny his request.

"May I use your phone?" Nolan asked my mother.

“Of course you can. Starr can show you where it is,” she said, as she quickly left the room to check on my father.

“That went a little better than I expected,” he remarked.

I put my wheels into motion and led him into the kitchen without saying anything. I was worried about Daddy. I wanted to go check on him as soon as Nolan’s phone call was being placed.

“Well, there it is. I’m gonna go see how he’s doing,” I said nodding to the backyard.

Nolan nodded as he picked up the receiver and began to dial. I made my way quickly out of the kitchen to the back door and shoved it open after a couple of tries. Dad was standing in the middle of the backyard with his hands in his pockets and staring up at the sky. I noticed that Mom was sitting on her chair swing just outside the door watching him. When she saw me go past her, she went inside.

"Hi Daddy," I said softly as I stopped next to him.

"You know I remember the day you were born," he replied. "You were so healthy and strong and perfect. I knew that you'd be my little girl forever; even after you got sick. Jane, I love you more than I can ever say, I just never thought this day would come. And it has nothing to do with your ... Situation. I just. No father ever thinks their little girl will leave them. No matter how silly it sounds."

"I'll always be your little girl. I'm just grown up now," I assured him softly.

"I meant what I said upstairs. You deserve to be happy. I'm glad that you said yes to Nolan, but you have to understand that I will never trust him. Not since the aquarium and I need you to accept that."

I put a hand on his leg. He looked down at me and I nodded. He let out a sigh and turned his attention back to the sky. I sat next to him in silence and watched the sky with him.

Ten minutes later, Stella ran out to announce that Nolan's parents had arrived.

Dad cleared his throat and straightened himself out before we went in. He held the door open for me and I made my way into the living room. His parents were sitting in the love seat talking to my mother and Nolan was sitting in his usual spot with Liam in his lap and Stella landing at his side.

"There you two are!" Mom said brightly. "Aaron, you remember Rosalie and Bryan don't you?"

Dad nodded and went to sit next to Mom. I was wheeling my way over there, when Nolan reached out an arm and stopped me. I glanced at him and he grinned as he pulled me backwards until I was sitting next to him. Liam climbed off of his lap and moved down the couch with Stella.

I raised an eyebrow when he stood up after a moment and lifted me out of the chair. He set me into the spot next to him and put his arm around me. I clasped my hands in my lap and leaned my head against his shoulder.

"Doesn't hurt does it?" he asked me quietly. I shook my head and he grinned again.

I felt that body heat starting to permeate throughout me again and I closed my eyes for a moment.

I loved feeling him so close.

"Nolan tells us that you have something you'd like to discuss with us," Bryan said to my father.

Dad explained everything to them. From the park to the aquarium to the proposal to his idea for living arrangements. By the end of it, Nolan's parents were looking at us very seriously.

"Are you sure this is something you both want to do? From the sounds of it, neither of you have been very responsible so far. Especially *you*," Bryan said looking pointedly at his son.

"Um, excuse me, Mr. ...Uh..."

It suddenly dawned on me that I had no idea what Nolan's last name was.

"Ransom," Nolan whispered.

I looked him incredulously.

"I swear it is," he whispered again laughing.

"Mr. Ransom." When his father didn't react any differently to mine being called Mr. East, I knew Nolan wasn't lying. "I understand where this can look bad, but I can't let Nolan take the blame for all of the unsafe things we did. I *am* a big girl and had I not wanted to do any of it, then I wouldn't have. He didn't have to coerce me into anything. And I think that the fact that he's been so careful with me and the fact that I can think for myself, speaks volumes of responsibility."

"While that may be, I think the two of you should *really* think about this. He has no history of ever interacting with someone ... in your position and I'm sure you've never dealt with someone as headstrong as my son can be."

"And what 'position' is that, Dad?" Nolan asked, removing his arm from around my shoulders and leaning forward.

"Son, all I'm saying is that people that are generally unhealthy only become unhealthier faster over time. Is that something you think you can deal with? "

I felt that flash of heat I felt whenever Nolan was near me go through me again. But ... He wasn't pressed against me so it finally dawned on me that it had never come from him. It had been coming from me.

And almost as if in some Shakespearean tragedy, I proved his father's point by losing consciousness and pitching forward onto the living room floor.

Nine

I woke up a day later, with my mother, father, and Nolan hovering over me in the hospital.

"What the hell happened?" I asked groggily.

"Your femur is infected. And because you didn't want the surgery, the infection quietly and quickly spread to your kidneys," Mom said tearfully.

"Oh. So what does that mean?"

"ESRD," my father said.

"What? That doesn't make sense. That happened way too fast," I said shaking my head.

"Your body isn't as strong as a healthy persons. It never has been since you got Legg–Calvé–Perthes Disease, Janey. Your body never fought the infection," he explained.

"Oh."

I didn't know how I felt about my new prognosis. I mean I wasn't mad and I wasn't glad. I was just *there.*

"So what's the next move?"

"Dialysis until they can find you a kidney," Mom said.

"Can I go home?"

"Not for a few days."

I looked over at Nolan who had said nothing so far, but looked like his world had just crashed down all around him.

"Do you want to stay here with me for a 'few days'? You're under no obligation of course," I joked with a weak smile.

"This is all my fault," he blurted out. "The infection is from when you had your accident at the aquarium. If I had just kept you in town and went to the damn zoo like I planned, you wouldn't be here right now."

He burst into tears as soon as he was done saying that. He put his face on my legs and was begging me to forgive him. I put my hand on his head and looked at my dad. I rolled my eyes good-naturedly and he forced a smile for my sake.

"Nolan, they're just kidneys. This happens to millions of people each year," I said, running my hands over his hair.

He blubbered something into my lap that I didn't understand and I just sighed. I didn't feel any sicker than I had been; just ungodly warm.

"Where are Nugget and Rabbit?" I asked my parents.

"They're with Nolan's parents down in the waiting room. Stella took one look at you and began to cry so hard that we had to move her out of the room. Liam said he would go with her to make sure she was okay."

I smiled. Liam was the best little brother in the world. He was always making sure that Stella and I were okay and threatening to beat up anyone who made us sad.

I still had the world's most emotional fiancée bawling into my lap when the nurse entered the room. She worked her way around him so that he didn't have to move. I watched her check my IV bag before switching it with a new one. I turned my head to the side when she brandished an ear thermometer. It beeped when it was done and she wrote down the information on a clipboard with an almost imperceptible head shake.

"How are you feeling, Jane?" she finally asked.

"Fine. I mean I don't feel anything abnormal. I'm just hot," I said.

"That happens with infections," she said nodding sympathetically. "I'm going to go let Dr. Ferrier know that you're awake now, hon. He's going to want you to sign those dialysis consent papers."

The mere mention of dialysis commanded another gut wrenching sob from Nolan.

“I’m not going to die, if that’s what’s got you so blubbery,” I said to him.

He looked up at me, his face beet red and tear stained. He took a couple of steadying breaths and then he spoke.

“I know. I’m not doubting your sustainability. I just hate that you’re here with a new problem because of me.”

“It was me too. I did say yes you know. Am I crying? No. Probably because I can’t afford to spare the fluid, but really. It’s okay. I’m okay. I’ll be okay.”

“Promise?” he asked.

“Promise.”

“Ms. East! Good to see you awake!”

A tall, young man with dark brown wavy hair and big blue eyes walked into the room. He was wearing a white lab coat and had a pair of glasses in his coat pocket. He was also holding a file and a clipboard. His face was very kind and it seemed to put everyone at ease.

"How are you feeling?" he asked coming to stand next to me.

Nolan got up and went into the bathroom to clean his face.

I shrugged, "About eighty five percent. Which is what I normally feel. Him on the other hand? Not so much."

My parents laughed and so did Dr. Ferrier. Nolan walked out of the bathroom armed to the teeth with tissue paper and came back to sit on the bed.

"I'm Nolan. Her fiancée," he said holding out a hand to the doctor.

"Please to meet you, young man. You have a very strong young lady here. I wouldn't worry about her too much. We've already put her name on the NFK list. It'll just be a waiting game, but with regular dialysis, I think her chances are pretty good."

He nodded and looked at me. I could see the smile on his face but the fear in his eyes shone brighter than any emotion I had seen before.

"Speaking of dialysis. If you would just take a moment to sign these forms consenting to the treatment, we can get you started right away," Dr. Ferrier said, placing the clipboard in my hands.

I skimmed the paper quickly out of habit, before I signed the first page. As I flipped it over to sign the second, I asked if someone could let Stella and Liam know that I was awake and okay. By the time I signed the fifth and final page, the kids entered the room. Stella hung by the door because she was scared to see me sick. At least that's what Liam said.

I handed the clipboard to the doctor who quickly walked out of the room to set everything up.

"Rabbit? Come here so I can see you," I called out.

"Are you still sick?" she called back.

“A little bit. But the doctor is going to make me all better. Come sit with me please,” I half begged.

I saw her small hand on the wall as she inched slowly forward, peeking her little terrified face around the corner. I smiled at her and her lower lip began to tremble. Nolan took a deep breath and left my side to go get her. His parents walked in behind her and watched him as he whispered to her that she and Liam were the first ones that I asked for and if she sat with me, I would be the happiest big sister in the world. She nodded and put her arms around his neck as he carried her over to my bed.

When he set her down and she turned her face to look at me, I almost cried. She looked so genuinely heartbroken and scared that for a moment, I considered changing my mind on the dialysis. She and Liam had gone through so much heartache with me being sick in their short lives that the best thing for them would probably be for me to die.

"I was scared," she said to me. Stella crawled up the length of the bed and laid down next to me, putting her arm around me again, like she did when we had our "sleepover."

"There's no reason to be scared, Rabbit. The doctor told me they're going to find new parts to make me all better soon and then we can all color in your room again. I'm not going anywhere."

If I had known that was the furthest thing from the truth, I would never have said it.

Ten

After three days of hospital grade dialysis, the doctor deemed I was well enough to go home. I would have to get dialysis three times a week until they found me some brand spanking new kidneys, and he instructed my parents not to let me do anything strenuous.

Nolan moved in immediately. He told his parents and mine that he refused to let another minute go by where he wasn't constantly with me. He also reasoned that it would be good "practice" for him to take me to dialysis, since we didn't know how long I would be waiting for new kidneys.

It was an impressive argument and it obviously worked.

So there I was lying in bed, staring at the ceiling when he finally entered the room and closed the door behind him securely. He opened his backpack and pulled out some kind of medical device I had never seen before.

"It's an osmoscope," he explained. "I was reading online when you were in the hospital about some holistic thing called Micro-Chinese Medicine Osmotherapy Treatment. Anyway, with these shredded herbs and this thingamajig, you won't need new kidneys and your ESRD should go away."

I smiled at him. Nolan had been as worried as my parents were and even though I hated to see them all like this, it was kind of refreshing to see someone other than them love me so much.

"Alright, so I'm going to have to flip you onto your stomach," he said after he got everything ready.

I nodded and turned myself over slowly. Nolan sat next to me on the bed and lifted the back of my shirt slowly. I closed my eyes when he traced his fingers over my bare skin slowly.

"What are you doing back there, buddy?" I asked playfully.

"Sorry. I just ... have I told you that you're beautiful?" he asked with a chuckle.

"Yes. Now medicate me please," I replied, my voice now muffled by the pillows.

The process was weird and it made my skin feel tingly. He apologized saying that he wished we were in a better environment than my room to do this in. I squirmed at the first couple of passes, but once I relaxed it was quite soothing. So much so, that I wound up taking a nice nap while he made his passes over my kidneys.

I woke up to Nolan snoring softly next to me. I lifted my head off of the pillows and looked at him groggily. I couldn't help but laugh; I had never watched him sleep before and his hair was all over the place. His mouth was slightly open, but other than that, he looked so peaceful.

"Huh?" he asked waking up slowly.

"Nice hair," I teased.

He gave me his half smile (and being that he was half asleep, it made him *that* much more irresistible) and pushed himself up onto his elbows.

"How you feeling?" he asked sleepily.

"I'm okay I guess. I mean I'm slightly less warm than before, but it could be because the window's open too. I don't know," I shrugged.

Nolan reached for me and lay back with my head against his chest.

"I don't expect it to work immediately. But I do expect *something.* I will accept a slight decrease in body temperature and discount the window being open as a factor," he murmured into my hair as he ran his hand up and down my back.

The doorknob started twisting and I sighed. I had a good thirty seconds of just lying there with him in silence, and it was like a warning went off somewhere in the house. "JANE AND

NOLAN ARE LYING IN BED TOGETHER. STOP THEM IMMEDIATELY BEFORE IT ESCALATES."

He slid out of the bed carefully and helped me roll onto my back. The doorknob jiggled again as he hurried to put his herbs and osmoscope into the backpack, before shoving it under my bed.

He cleared his throat and made his way to the door. He gave me a glance and I nodded.

Liam was standing there waiting patiently. When Nolan opened the door for him, he reached down and picked up a food tray that he had been holding and came over to the bed.

"Let me help you with that, kiddo," Nolan said. He held the food tray so that Liam could climb onto the bed, and then handed it back to him as he knelt next to me.

"I made you my favorite, Starr. Peanut butter and jelly!" he said proudly.

I looked down at the hopelessly sloppy sandwich and grinned. I saw the silver colored juice pouch sitting next to the sandwich and looked at him.

"I can have one of your juices too?"

"Yeah! That's what makes the sandwich so good. The juice," he replied reaching for the pouch.

"Help me sit up?" I asked Nolan.

He slid me up gently and in a manner where he wouldn't have to move Liam from the bed or so that he wouldn't have to remove the food tray. Once I was situated, I watched Liam as he carefully peeled the straw off the back out the pouch and began the task of poking in through the hole. It took him a few frustrated tries, but once he got it, he gave me the biggest smile.

"Thanks Nugget!" I said as he handed it to me.

I took a sip.

Fruit Punch, his favorite.

"I tried to cut your sandwich in half but Mom told me that I couldn't use the knife. So I ripped it in half for you," he said holding out half.

I grinned when I saw where his small fingers had punctured the bread and its contents. I took a big bite and he grinned happily.

"I'm gonna go make you one too, Nolan," he said suddenly hopping off of the bed and running out of the room.

We both laughed. Liam was such a good kid and I loved him so much. I don't know where he got his strength from but if I could just get one tenth of it, I knew I'd be okay.

About five minutes later, he came in juggling another sloppy pb&j sandwich and juice pouch. He handed them both to Nolan and pulled himself up onto the bed.

I finished my sandwich and Nolan downed his in two bites. The three of us sat there quietly while I drank my juice and Nolan shared his with Liam.

"You look really pretty today, Starr," Liam observed. "It's almost like you're not sick."

"Thanks, Nugget," I replied pulling him into a hug.

"I asked Daddy and Mommy if I could give you my kidneys. They said I'm not big enough," he said sadly.

"What?" I asked in surprise.

"My kidneys; I want to give them to you, but I'm not big enough."

"Liam, look at me," I said very seriously. "I want you to know that you are the best brother in the entire world. You want to do so much for me and you don't even worry or care if it will make you sick too. I promise that I will try to get better as soon as I can so that you don't have to worry about me anymore. If I don't, please don't ever think it was your fault or that you could have done more. It's just what happens to some people."

"But it's not a'sposed to happen to *you*," he argued, bursting into tears.

I held him tightly and let him cry into my chest. Nolan reached between us and pulled out the food tray and left the room. Silently, I was thankful to have this time alone with Liam. He and Stella had been wrecks since I had fallen at PPG and I felt terrible for doing that to them.

"Liam, what on Earth?" Mom asked rushing into the room.

"He's just sad is all," I explained, still hugging him.

"Why?" she asked coming over to sit on the bed.

"Because he's not big enough to give me his kidneys. He wanted to give me his legs for my birthday, you know," I said quietly.

"Oh sweetheart," she said collecting Liam from my arms and cradling him in hers. "Starr is going to be fine, Liam. Especially because she has you for a brother."

I watched her get up and leave with him. I honestly wish she wouldn't have said that. If I didn't get kidneys in time, I didn't want him to think it was his fault that I died.

I turned my face to look out the window. That was the first time in all of my life, that I finally faced the prospect of mortality. The ESRD diagnosis didn't count, because I was kind of out of it when they told me. But now, with Liam angry with himself for not being able to give me his kidneys and Nolan trying holistic treatments to "save" me, I knew that everyone was worried.

Eleven

There was a soft knock at the door that took my attention away from the basically commuted death sentence. It was Nolan and he was leaning against the door frame looking at me curiously.

“Is it okay if I come back in?” he asked.

“Always,” I replied, forcing a smile.

He walked over and climbed into the bed with me. I inhaled his scent and closed my eyes. (For some reason, Nolan always smelled slightly of autumn fields.)

“What’s wrong, Janey?” he asked into my neck, where he had nuzzled his face.

“I’m just worried about Liam. If I don’t make it, he’s going to have a very hard time. I don’t want him to blame himself. Especially when there’s nothing he can do about it,” I confided.

"What makes you think you're going anywhere?" he asked, tightening his grip around my waist.

"Nothing really. I just ... if anything happens, will you please look out for Liam and Stella? They're both going to be destroyed."

"Promise."

I intertwined my fingers with his and turned my face to look at him. He was looking at me with a sad smile and I leaned over and kissed him softly.

"Thank you."

"Can I ask you something?" he asked.

I nodded.

"Who's going to look out for *me* if something happens to you?"

Truth be told, I hadn't thought about that. I figured he was an adult and he'd be able to mourn and move on.

"Not to sound callous," I stared slowly, "But you'll forget about me eventually. They won't."

He let out a scoff and rolled onto his back. He pulled his arm away from me and stared at the ceiling for a moment before speaking again.

"Speaking of forgetting about you," he said, slightly bitter, "I have something I want to do for you. Or should I just leave now and start 'forgetting'?"

I turned on my side and looked at him.

"Nolan, they're *children.* All I meant is that it's going to be way harder on them than anyone else. Including my parents. And this is even if I go anywhere, which I have no plans of doing," I said becoming frustrated.

"Promise me that you won't," he said suddenly.

I stayed quiet. That wasn't something I could promise because I wasn't sure about it.

"Janey. Promise me," he said again.

I nodded, "Promise."

He sat up and began to fish around in his pockets until he found what he was looking for.

When he found it, he stood up and went to the other side of the bed and carefully sat me up.

"Rabbit! Nugget! Come here please!" he called out.

Stella came running in with fresh flowers from Mom's garden and Liam, still red faced, came in holding a big box.

Nolan grinned at them and they sprang into action. They climbed the bed and each stood up behind me to help me sit up without feeling much pain and held their gifts on either side of me.

"Ready!" they said together.

I looked at them suspiciously. They both wore big grins on their faces; even Liam.

"MOMMY! DADDY! COME ON!" Stella bellowed.

"You've got quite a set of lungs on you," I said wincing.

She giggled and I smiled.

"Okay, ready," Mom said.

I turned and saw that she and Dad were standing on either sides of the room with cameras in their hands.

Nolan nodded at them and looked down at me.

"Remember when I read you that birthday card and asked you to marry me?" he asked.

I nodded.

"That was kind of spur of the moment, you know? I just decided to say what was on my mind, and I'll tell you this much, Janey. I haven't changed my mind about it. So, I thought I'd be a little more traditional about it."

He pulled me to my feet and the kids rushed forward and put their hands on my back, using all of their strength to hold me up. I looked up at him in confusion. He simply smiled and dropped down on one knee.

My hand went to my mouth and my eyes watered.

A camera flash went off. I looked over in the direction and my mom smiled.

"Jane *Camille* East", he started with a mischievous grin, "I never thought that I would find anyone that I would want to spend my life with. I've never been the life-spending-with type of guy. But there's something about you; something special, something that was clear in the pictures I saw of you. Something that tells me that I need to spend my life with you, something that tells me that someone like you truly does come along once in a lifetime. You *get* me, Janey and no one has before you. I can't help that I love you as much as I do. I really can't and I don't want to. So, while the kids still have enough strength to hold you up, let me wrap this up by asking you a question." (I found myself stifling a giggle. Stella and Liam were starting to have a hard time holding me up, which was evident in my body beginning to sway.) Nolan opened his hand and presented me with a beautiful antique, sapphire ring. “Will you marry me, kid?” he finally asked.

Another flash went off and this time it came from Dad’s direction. I didn’t look though. I was too busy staring down at the one person besides my family that made me feel loved and wanted; the one person that didn’t care that I clearly wasn’t like everyone else.

“This is the part where you say yes,” Stella whispered into my ear.

I looked at her and smiled. Then I turned to Liam.

“What do you think?” I whispered to him.

“Say yes,” he half whispered, half grunted back.

“Well, they kids seem to approve of you,” I said, eyeing Nolan. “My answer is yes. Today, tomorrow, and forever; my answer will be yes.”

Nolan’s grin widened as he slid the ring onto my ring finger. He got to his feet and took my face in his hands.

"I got it from here guys," he said to Stella and Liam, without looking at them.

They fell back against the bed and hooted and hollered as Nolan kissed me. Passionately, deeply, with everything that he had inside of him.

The camera flashes were almost nonstop and I felt like my room had suddenly acquired strobe lights. After what seemed like forever, we broke apart and he held me tightly against him.

"I love you, Janey," he whispered into my ear.

"And I you, Nolan."

"Promise?" he asked softly.

"Promise."

"Stop kissing already! We've got presents for you," Stella suddenly yelled.

The adults in the room laughed as he helped me back onto my bed. Nolan propped me up against the headboard and I asked him to pull the sheets up over my legs.

"I got you flowers," Stella said pulling her little bouquet apart and handing half to me and half to him.

"Thanks, Rabbit," I said giving her a hug.

"You're welcome," she said.

"I got you some toys," Liam said pulling the lid off of his mystery box.

I raised an eyebrow as he reached into the box and pulled out his two favorite possessions in the world. He handed me his baseball glove and handed Nolan his favorite action figure; *Iron Man.*

"Thank you, Nugget," I said softly, hugging him tightly.

He smiled proudly and gave Nolan a hug before he went to join his sister next to our parents.

"We've got something for you two as well. We're just waiting on Rosalie and Bryan to get here," Mom said mysteriously.

“Guys, it’s not like we just got married. We just got engaged again,” I protested with a laugh.

Mom and Dad exchanged a grin. Dad got my wheelchair and hoisted me off of the bed and into it.

“To the living room, everyone! They should be here soon,” he said.

Twenty minutes later, Nolan’s parents knocked on the door. Mom let them in and they went and sat on the love seat, which was pretty much next to my parents.

The four of them looked at each other with grins before they turned to us.

“I kind of feel like I’m going to get devoured or something. This is getting creepy,” Nolan leaned over and whispered to me.

“Yeah; I can see what you’re saying. The cannibalistic tendencies are becoming quite apparent these days,” I whispered back.

“You goof!” he said as he began to laugh.

I winked at him and turned my attention back to the four people that were watching us closely.

"We actually drew straws to find out who would get to tell you this," Bryan said finally with a laugh. "And I pulled the lucky one."

He stood up and cleared his throat. He walked over to us and placed an envelope on the couch arm between us.

"Before you open that, we just want you to know that even though we still have some doubts, for medical reasons only, we're very happy for the two of you. Okay. Open it," he said sitting down and leaning forward.

"Should we draw straws to see who opens it?" Nolan asked.

"We could, but I don't have any straws. However we could each just grab and end and rip it open," I reasoned.

"Seems fair. Let's do it," he said handing me the envelope.

"On the count of three?" I asked, to which he nodded. "One, two, three!"

We each ripped our halves of the envelope and a pair of keys fell out onto the carpet. He leaned down and picked them up, giving our parents a curious look.

"We got you your own place!" Mom all about yelled in excitement. "The rent has been prepaid for a year; to give you guys some financial help for a bit. We thought it was the best thing to do. What do you think?"

We both sat there in shock. I looked at Nolan doubtfully and he returned my look.

"Mom. Are you sure this is okay?" I asked her.

"Of course it is. You're both adults and you're going to have to live on your own eventually. Aaron was the last one to come around on it, but the four us agree that if you're going to start a life together, you should *live* together; alone."

"Do you understand the responsibility that's going to come with this, Nolan?" Mr. Ransom asked him seriously.

"Yes. And I hope you all know that you can trust me to do an amazing job. I want a long life with Jane, so I'll take care of her as best as I can," he replied squeezing my hand.

"There's something else you should know," Rosalie said.

We both looked at her expectantly.

"You'll be living in Morningside."

I raised an eyebrow, "But there is no Morningside in Ohio."

"We know," Dad said softly. "It's five minutes away from PPG."

"What about her dialysis?" Nolan asked leaning forward.

"It's all taken care of. We had her information transferred to one of the best Nephrologists in all of Pennsylvania," Mom said.

I was still looking at my father who was dangerously close to tears. I let go of Nolan and rolled over to my dad and hugged him harder than I ever had before.

He held me and we both became racked with sobs.

It was as if though we knew that would be the last time we would ever see each other again.

Twelve

Three months later, I was sitting out in our backyard, watching Nolan doing some yard work. When our parents said that we had our own place, they failed to mention that it was a house; a bungalow with a wide front porch and acres of property.

As he turned the riding mower around and began to make another pass, I had to admit that I was absolutely impressed with him. He had taken on the responsibility of taking me to dialysis; always arriving twenty minutes early and sitting with me through the entire thing. He also kept up his holistic treatments on me faithfully.

His twenty third birthday was next Friday and I had already plotted and schemed with our families to throw him a party. I didn't know how he would react to it, but he had done so much for me that I wanted to give him one day of being a "normal" person. One day of not having to take care of someone else. One day where I would get to take care of *him.*

I know this sounds odd when I say it, but he had definitely grown into a man in the time that we lived together away from our parents.

He worked a full time job close to home, so that if I ever needed him or if there was an emergency of some kind, he wouldn't be far away.

After his hard days of contracting work, (Daddy managed to get him a job with a notable company in Morningside), he would still find the strength to help me get into the bathtub and into bed at night.

The bathing thing was particularly odd to me considering that I was still a virgin. If he was or was not, I never asked, because I liked to believe that we would be each other's first everything one day. Anyway, I wasn't a virgin by my choosing. I think it was a combination of things. Him being tired most of the time, my being in a wheelchair, and of course, a touch of ESRD. Throw in his fear of further fracturing my femur and I was pretty certain that I would be dying an unsexed, kidney failing, brittle boned, chair bound champion. Again, not by choice.

But, as I watched his sweat body glistening in the hot afternoon sun, my hormones reminded me to call my Orthopedist and my Nephrologist. I was bound and determined to make his twenty third birthday as memorable as possible.

I turned my chair around and rolled through the back door to let myself in. Luckily, the kitchen wasn't far from the door, so I was able to quickly retrieve his gallon jug of cold water and take it back out to him in no time.

"Thanks Janey," he said with a tired smile.

"You're welcome," I replied. "Why don't you take a break? Come sit with me in the shade."

He nodded and took a big swig of his water while he followed me across the yard to the lone and quite large maple tree. It was the only tree in our yard and we both loved the damn thing almost as much as we loved each other.

Underneath the tree were two reclinable lawn chairs. There was also a hammock that he hadn't set up yet. Partially because he was afraid that by some act of God, it would snap and fall with both of us in it, and mean my untimely demise.

He yawned loudly as he laid down and closed his eyes. Almost immediately, he opened his eyes and gave me a sheepish grin.

"Sorry," he said as he started to push himself up.

I gave him a playful shove back into his chair.

"With as hard as this may be to believe, I *am* capable of lifting myself into that chair," I said dryly.

"I don't mind doing it," he replied quickly, pushing himself up again.

"Nolan, if you get out of that chair to help me, I swear you'll be talking to yourself for the next few days," I warned, leaning down to lock the wheels. (My father had the new locks installed shortly after my spill at PPG.)

I leaned toward the recliner chair as he held it in place and I pulled myself out of my wheelchair and into the recliner. I winced a little at the pain of dropping into it, before I straightened out my legs and leaned back.

"So, have you thought about what you want for your birthday?" I asked conversationally.

He took another swig of water.

"Um, no. I honestly haven't thought about it."

I rolled my eyes. Of course he hadn't. He was too busy working and then coming home to work some more.

The house phone rang interrupting our brief conversation and he moved to get up.

"Stay there. I can answer it," I said reaching for my chair.

"Jane, it's not a big deal," he replied.

"Exactly. So you stay *there* and let me get it," I said pulling myself into my chair and unlocking the wheels.

"Hey," he said, as I started to turn the chair.

I looked at him and raised an eyebrow. He reached for me and rolled me within inches of him.

"I love you," he whispered simply.

I smiled shyly, "I love you too."

"How did I get so lucky?" he asked, before leaning forward and kissing me. It was his gentle and I would like to think world renowned, I-don't-know-what-I'd-do-without-you kiss, before pulling away and letting me roll into the house.

I managed to grab the phone just as the answering machine clicked on.

"Hello?" I asked breathlessly.

"Jane?" It was Dr. Bright, my Orthopedist. I liked him a lot. The fact that his last name was Bright only made him that much more likable.

"Hey, Dr. Bright!"

"I've got some good news for you," he said cheerfully. "The iron and calcium supplements we've been having you take are strengthening your femur. The pain you've been feeling should be going away fairly soon."

"That's great news!" I said enthusiastically.

"Well, I just wanted to let you know and to tell you to keep up the good work!"

"Wait, Dr. Bright? There's something I want to ask you," I said nervously.

"Sure," he said.

Well, here goes nothing.

"Am I strong enough … would it be possible for me to … um … engage in … activities?" I asked, stumbling over my words.

"Well, I'm sure there are a number of things you can do while your bones strengthen. What kind of particular activity did you have in mind?" Dr. Bright asked pleasantly.

"Nolan's birthday is next week and I wanted to …," my voice trailed off.

"OH! Oh I see! I honestly wouldn't suggest it until your bones have healed. If you'd like to come in tomorrow, we can do a couple of tests and see what, if anything, you'd be able to do for that activity," he said kindly.

Tomorrow was Friday, so Nolan would be at work, which meant that I could take the bus to the doctor's office and do my tests without him knowing.

"That would be fine, Dr. Bright. What time tomorrow?" I asked.

"I'll transfer you to the nurse and you can work out a good time with her. I'll see you tomorrow, Jane," he said before transferring me.

I hung up the phone five minutes later. I was set for a nine a.m. appointment with Dr. Bright.

I spun my chair around and screamed. Nolan was leaning against the kitchen counter giving me a tired smile.

"Sorry, I didn't mean to scare you. I just came in because the heat was making more tired," he said, punctuating his sentence with a yawn. "I didn't mean to eavesdrop either, but why do you need to go see Dr. Bright tomorrow?"

"You know that nuclear blast of iron and calcium that he keeps giving me? Apparently it's doing good things in the femur department."

"That's awesome!" he said happily.

"Between you and me, I feel like I can do just about anything," I said with a grin.

"I'm sure you can, Janey. Now all we need is a phone call from Dr. Kowalski saying that they've either found some kidneys for you or that you're kidneys are healing, and I'll be the happiest man in the world."

"I planned on calling her today," I replied rolling my eyes.

He wasn't going to be happy until I was one hundred percent better, even though he knew that my personal best had always been eight five percent.

"Don't be mad at me, Janey. I just hate that you got worse because of *me*," he said quietly.

I took a deep breath and mustered all the patience that I possibly could.

"Nolan, I'm not mad. You have to understand that my having ESRD is ultimately my own fault. I chose not to have the surgery and so the infection spread. My fault; not yours. Me falling down the steps at PPG? Accident; no one's fault. I need you to stop blaming yourself for shit that you *did not do.*"

He cleared his throat, but didn't say anything. Instead, he looked like an angry little boy that had just been scolded.

And I couldn't help but laugh.

He reminded me of Liam when Mom or Dad would say the magical words, "time out."

Suddenly, he walked past me and grabbed the phone. I moved to the side to give him space, but he pulled me back toward him.

"Yes, hi. This is Nolan Ransom; I was looking for Dr. Kowalski please." He paused for a moment. "Right, in regards to Jane East."

"What are you doing?" I asked quietly.

He held up a hand before he spoke into the phone again, "Hi Dr. Kowalski. It's Nolan. Yeah I have her here with me. I'm gonna put you on speaker, hold on."

He hit the button and placed the phone on the small island in the kitchen.

"Okay, we're here," he said.

"Hello Jane! How are you feeling?" Dr. Kowalski asked.

"I'm fine. I'm so sorry if we bothered you. We were just wondering if there's any news," I said.

"Unfortunately we haven't heard from the NKF yet. I also haven't gotten your last test results back," she said apologetically.

"Oh. Okay. Sorry again for bothering you," I said dejectedly.

"Dr. Kowalski, there was something else that I think Jane wanted to ask you," Nolan said, grabbing onto my chair again.

"Shoot Jane," she said kindly.

I looked at him questioningly.

"I told you that I didn't mean to eavesdrop," he said lowering his voice and covering the receiver, "But I heard what you asked Dr. Bright."

My face drained of color and I felt completely embarrassed. He walked around behind me and put his arms around my shoulders. Resting his chin on my shoulder, he gave me a soft kiss on the neck.

"I love you, no matter what. You know that, don't you? I don't want you to hurt yourself for something you think I need or deserve or whatever your reason is."

"Hello?"

I pulled away from him and grabbed the phone. I took Dr. Kowalski off of speaker and put the phone to my ear.

"How safe would it be for me to have sex?" I asked bluntly.

"Having ESRD doesn't affect your sex life. I know most people think it does, but it doesn't," she responded. "I would check with Dr. Bright about the femur, though."

"I already talked to him. Thanks Dr. Kowalski and sorry again for bothering you."

"My patients are never a bother," she said before hanging up.

I hung up with her and turned put a hand to my face for a moment. I was angry that Nolan had taken away my element of surprise, but I understood why he did it.

"Dr. Kowalski said that failing kidneys don't affect the sex life. Dr. Bright is going to run some tests on me tomorrow to see if my bones are strong enough. I'm gonna go take a nap now. Suddenly I have a massive headache," I grumbled wheeling past him.

I decided to take my angry nap on the living room couch.

Nolan decided to follow me.

I pulled myself onto the couch and stretched out.

Nolan moved my wheelchair to the end of the couch.

I put an arm over my face.

Nolan grabbed and draped a sheet around me.

"Will you cut it out?" I exploded angrily.

He jumped and looked at me in surprise. I had never, in the entire time we had been together, yelled at him. Any arguments we almost had were always swayed by goofy grins or rock, paper, scissor.

"What did I do?" he asked incredulously.

"You treat me like I'm an *invalid.* I can't stand that! I was perfectly capable of moving the damn wheelchair and grabbing the sheet, if I wanted one to begin with," I said in frustration.

He took a deep, steadying breath and held up a fist with his eyes closed. I sighed. He was right; there was no reason to argue. Unless fate decided otherwise.

We both shook our fists three times and played our hands.

To win by rock (which he did) meant the argument was over. To win by scissor meant separate rooms. To win by paper, meant we slept in said separate rooms that night.

He sat down in his leather recliner across from me and looked at me for a moment. I was expecting another rousing game of RPS when I saw the half smile starting to creep over his face.

“Why?” he asked curiously.

“Why what?” I asked, putting my arm back over my face.

“You know what.”

I turned my head and looked at him.

“I am under the assumption, albeit possibly the wrong assumption, that you have never had ... an encounter. Don’t tell me if you have! I live in a rather glorious parallel universal where you haven’t!” I said raising a hand. “For some reason, my hormones have been flying out of control lately, and with your birthday being in eight days, I figured it would be an opportune time.”

Nolan was quiet. He had turned his gaze away from me when I was presenting my reasons, maintaining some kind of eye lock on something outside.

"Can I go with you to your appointment tomorrow?" he finally asked without looking at me.

"If you want. I was just going to take the bus there and back."

He got up from his chair, walked over to me, and kissed my forehead.

"Take your nap, Janey. I'm gonna call my boss and tell him that I can't make it in tomorrow."

Thirteen

Friday, June 28th

Nolan pulled into the parking lot of Dr. Bright's office and got as close to the front door as he could. I knew it would make life a lot easier if I just broke down and got a handicap sticker, but I refused to get one. I reasoned that the people that really needed those spaces should have them; not someone like me who was in almost perfect eighty five percent health and could make it to the door just fine.

He pulled my wheelchair out of the back of his SUV and came around once it was open and ready for me.

I pushed open the door and pulled myself out. Nolan took over and lowered me into the seat. I looked up at him and raised my face for a kiss. He grinned and obliged before we went into the office.

I smiled at Cori, the young and bubbly, raven-haired receptionist as Nolan signed me in. She gave me a big smile and wave, as she handed him a clipboard. I went into the waiting room and found a spot furthest away from the entrance so that no one would be blocked on the way in and out.

A few moments later, he came over and sat down next to me with the clipboard and a pen.

"So, Ms. East, besides being engaged to the devastatingly handsome Nolan Ransom, what else have you been up to since we've last seen you?" he asked in a faux Hollywood reporter voice.

I raised an eyebrow at him and he held up the clipboard. It was a questionnaire. He balanced it on his knee and began to quietly ask me the questions on it. I rested my head on his shoulder while I answered.

For some reason, I had been particularly tired that day when I woke up. I chalked it up to the five hour "nap" I had taken earlier in the day. Too much sleep has a tendency to make you tired. At least that's what I remember reading somewhere.

By the time we were done with the questionnaire, I felt like I could nap again. Nolan went over and handed the clipboard to Cori. When he sat down next to me again, he took my hand in his and turned his attention to the television in the high left corner of the room.

Ten minutes later, Angela the head nurse, came out and called my name.

"Do you want me to go with you?" Nolan asked.

"Yeah, could you push me too please?" I asked yawning.

"Wow, you *must* be tired," he replied playfully as he guided me down the hallway and into exam room three.

I shrugged as he plucked me out of my chair and laid me down on the examination bed. He stood there for a moment, his hands on either side of me, smiling.

The door opened and in walked Dr. Bright. One of the tallest, kindest, gray haired, glasses wearing men in all of existence.

“Hello young friends!” he said cheerfully.

Nolan moved away from me and shook the doctor’s hand, before having a seat in the chair next to where I was laying.

“Everything looks good,” he said sitting in his stool and glancing over the questionnaire. I watched him lift the second page and glance at me after reading about half way down. “When did you start becoming fatigued?”

“Oh about when I woke up this morning,” I joked.

“Honestly Jane,” he said kindly, but firmly.

I shrugged, “’Bout a week ago.”

"Why didn't you say anything?" Nolan asked glancing at me.

"Considering what you all day and what you come home to do, I have no right to complain about being tired more often than not," I replied dryly.

Dr. Bright looked at us in turn, before putting the clipboard down.

"Do you know why she's here today?" he asked Nolan.

"Yeah, I overheard her on the phone with you."

"And what do you think?"

"I don't think she do something she thinks I want or need or whatever," he answered.

"That was a lot of thinking going on there guys," I joked.

"This is very serious Jane," Dr. Bright said. "I'm going to perform a small battery of tests on you. I'm going to need you to be honest with me about the pain level, if there is any. I won't know if I can tell you to go ahead with this if you aren't honest."

I nodded.

Dr. Bright came over and put his hands on my stomach.

"Ready?" he asked me.

I nodded again and he gently pushed down. It didn't hurt, so I shook my head. He moved his hands down further, to my lower stomach and pressed down again. While it was a bit uncomfortable, it wasn't pain mention worthy.

I shook my head again.

Next he moved his hand to my right thigh and watched my face carefully as he pushed down. I winced a little and held up three fingers. He nodded and went to make a note on his clipboard.

He came back and went to the left side of the bed. I instinctively reached out for Nolan's hand.

That was the "bad" side.

The infected femur of septic death side.

"Are you ready?" Dr. Bright asked softly.

I closed my eyes and nodded.

He pushed down. The lights exploded illuminating the darkness I had just submerged myself into and I squeezed the ever loving shit out of Nolan's hand.

Dr. Bright moved his hands away and sighed. But there was something he was aware of. That even though that hurt, a lot, it wasn't as bad as it usually was.

"Jane?" he prompted. "I need a number."

I took a couple of quick breaths and let go of Nolan's hand. I held up five fingers on that hand and three on the other.

"An eight? Are you sure?" he asked me in surprise.

"Yeah," I replied breathing shakily. "It didn't hurt as bad as it did the last time you did it when we were here."

Dr. Bright made a couple of additional notes in my file, which he had under the clipboard, before turning back to us.

"Jane, you're a virgin, correct?" he asked. I nodded. "And you, Nolan?"

I turned my face and closed my eyes. I didn't want his answer to destroy my fantasy world.

"Yes," he said rather loudly.

I whipped my head to look at him in surprise.

He laughed, "Parallel universe intact?"

"Only if you're telling the truth," I said narrowing my eyes.

"It's the truth," he said shyly.

"Guys? You can discuss this later. The reason I asked is because I need to explain something to you about why I don't feel comfortable saying yes to this. One moment please," he said getting up and leaving the room.

I looked at the ceiling trying to think of what he could say that would justify telling us that we'd never be able to physically love each other.

I sighed when the door opened and closed again. I glanced at Dr. Bright and saw him holding two skeletal pelvic bone models. I glanced at Nolan who was leaned forward looking at them curiously.

"When two people have sex, there is a lot of pelvic movement," Dr. Bright said sitting down. "Essentially, with the amount of thrusting that you will be doing, your pelvic bones will be coming in contact a lot."

He tilted the larger bone to demonstrate. My face turned bright red.

"Now, your femur is located in your pelvic bone. Healthy femurs can obviously take this; unhealthy femurs cannot. Do you understand why I can't say yes?" he asked looking at me.

"No," I replied bluntly.

Dr. Bright sighed heavily and set the molds down on the small table. He ran a hand over his face and looked at me.

"Alright, if you're strong enough to stand on your two feet, then you're strong enough for sex," he said finally.

I looked at him defiantly. Nolan was giving me a sad smile, but I had a surprise for both of them. I used my hands to push myself up to a seated position and then swung my legs around the side of the bed. I looked down at the floor a little apprehensively because I was going to have to *hop* down, which meant landing on my feet.

I took a deep breath and lowered myself as far as I could onto my right foot. Nolan instinctively moved forward but I waved him away. He hovered for a moment until I gave him an annoyed look.

Once my right foot was securely on the ground, I lowered my left one gingerly. It hurt like holy hell, but I had a point to prove. I shifted all the weight that I could into my right leg and pushed myself away from the bed.

Even though my left leg was slightly bent, I still had my foot touching the floor.

"Good enough?" I asked Dr. Bright.

"No, but I have a feeling that you're not going to listen to me anyway," he replied with a small smile.

"Janey, how did you do that?" Nolan asked as I pulled myself back onto the bed.

"I've been practicing when you've been at work," I admitted proudly.

He didn't look too happy about that, but I figured he would get over it. After all, he couldn't possibly think that I would just sit around in my chair and not do anything all day.

"I expected this," Dr. Bright said reaching for my file. "I need you to sign this paper. It's an AMA release."

I asked Nolan to hand me the clipboard and I signed the document. He handed it back to Dr. Bright and we were on our way home.

Fourteen

Saturday, June 29th

I spent most of the night listening to a lecture. Nolan told me that while he was beyond proud of me, he was upset that I had been forcing myself to stand because that could possibly disrupt my healing process, and if I fell, I'd have no way of getting to the phone to let him know.

The next morning when I woke up, I was in a vice grip. The kind of grip that said *I don't trust you enough to not try to walk to your chair.*

So I laid there and stared at the ceiling for another twenty minutes until he woke up. And when he did, he brushed his lips against my neck, his hair tickling my face.

My frustration at being semi restrained went away and I smiled. He loosened the grip around my waist and pressed his lips a little harder against my neck. I felt something weird happening inside of me as he gently rubbed his hand across my waist, before throwing the blankets off of us.

Six days ahead of schedule, I had my first physical experience with the man that I loved. It was awkward because he did his best not to hurt me (the femur situation mostly) and because he insisted that I stay on my back. It didn't particularly last very long and it wasn't particularly spectacular, but it was with *Nolan* and that made it absolutely perfect.

We laid there breathing heavily and slightly sweat covered. He had me pulled close to him as we stared at the ceiling and I did my best to put my new nagging femur pain in the back of my mind.

"Wow," he finally said.

I laughed.

"Thank you," he said.

"For what?" I asked, turning my head to look at him.

"For being you. I don't think I've ever thanked you for that. I swear I wouldn't trade a day with you for anything in the world. And, no, that's not the after sex talking," he replied with a chuckle. But then he grew serious.

"There's something I have to confess."

"Okay."

He let out a sigh, "Remember how I told you that I fell in love with you when I saw that picture of you holding Liam and hugging Stella?"

I nodded.

"Well, before that, your parents were telling us about your condition and I ... I didn't want to do it. I didn't want to go to their house and I didn't want to even *try* to be your friend. I had never had a friend in your situation and I was worried I was either going to say something stupid or hurt your feelings in some way. I think Aaron could see it as it settled on my face; the refusal. That's why he pulled out the pictures. To show me that just because you were in a wheelchair, you weren't any less normal.

"So when he took out his wallet and the cascade of pictures came flying out, I was intrigued. I took his wallet and went through the pictures like I told you before, but my mind hadn't changed until I saw that picture.

"Your big, proud awkward smile and your holding a newborn Liam and still making Stella feel loved ... I had to meet the beautiful girl with the big heart," he finished wistfully.

I didn't say anything. Partly because there was nothing to say and partly because I didn't know *what* to say.

Nolan had seen me as everyone else had at first. A girl in a wheelchair who probably needed round the clock care.

"Please tell me that you didn't feel bad for me," I finally said.

"No. I didn't."

"Good. Thank you."

We were silent for a few moments when he turned on his side.

He brushed my hair off of my face and behind my ear. I smiled as he looked into my eyes and ran his finger down the side of my face.

"Can I tell you what I want for my birthday now?"

I raised my eyebrows and waited.

"What I want is for you to be my wife. On my birthday. When our family is here, I want to make it official."

I didn't know what to say. I wanted to scream yes, I really did, but I couldn't get over the fact really that he didn't want to have anything to do with me at first.

"Well? Do you want to go from Ms. East to Mrs. Ransom on Friday? Or Mrs. East-Ransom?" he asked making a goofy face.

"Mrs. Ransom will do just fine," I answered softly.

“Good. I was hoping so,” he said happily as he climbed out of the bed.

The rest of the day followed The Routine. I waited in bed while he showered. When he was done he came to get me and help me into the bath chair. As per usual, he sat down next to the tub and began to flip through magazines.

He sighed when the phone rang and got to his feet.

“I’ll be right back. Just holler if you need anything,” he said through the shower curtain.

“I’m just showering. I doubt anything earthshattering will happen while you’re gone,” I teased.

Nolan laughed as he walked out of the bathroom.

As I shampooed my hair, I started to feel warm again, followed by a pain flair up. I put a hand to my side and winced as the pain slowly started to become more prominent.

I took labored breaths and tried to ignore it as I started to desperately wash the shampoo out of my hair.

"Nolan?" I asked through clenched teeth.

No response. He was still on the phone.

"Ow!" I whined quietly, as the pain shot through to my other side.

I pulled the curtain back and turned myself in the chair. I put my hands on the sides of the tub and began to pull myself out.

Something was terribly wrong and for the first time in my life, I wanted help. And I wanted it more than anything I had ever wanted before.

"Nolan?" I said a little louder.

I heard him laughing on the phone. I managed to pull myself onto the rug on the bathroom floor and I grabbed the magazine he had left on the floor, flinging it as hard as I could through the open door.

"What the hell? Hey, I'll call you back," I heard him say as he replaced the receiver.

"Jane?" he asked, making his way back to the bathroom.

I lay my head on the rug and tilted my face toward the door. I saw his sneakers come around the corner. I saw them stop and then I saw them pick up speed as he flew into the bathroom and picked me up in his arms.

"I'm sorry," I managed to whisper as another shock of pain went through me.

"You're going to be okay. I'm gonna call the ambulance right now," he said in a shaky voice.

He laid me down on the living room couch and reached over the coffee table to get his cell phone off of the entertainment center.

My vision was starting to blur as the exquisite pain began to control ever last part of me.

"Hello? I need help! My wife she has kidney problems and leg problems and ... I found her on the bathroom floor almost passed out. Please just send someone!" he yelled desperately into the phone.

The operator said something to him. He yelled something back in frustration.

Funny how all things audible are now going away.

Nolan ran from the room and came back with a dress. I knew it was because he didn't want me to be embarrassed about being naked when the paramedics arrived and because he didn't want to move me more than he had to.

I saw a blob hovering over me so I closed my eyes. I knew it was him but I wasn't able to see him properly and it scared me.

Vision leaving; check.

My kidneys were obviously in shut down mode. I remembered reading online that when your kidneys shut down all types of neat things happen. You can't speak; you lose your vision and hearing.

They were done working and I was starting lose consciousness.

I felt tears rolling down the sides of my face. It wasn't because I was scared; it was because I was tired. Tired of fighting, tired of trying to be normal, tired of trying to be everything that I wasn't.

I closed my eyes and hoped that of all the things in the world that could possibly happen, that I would at least get to see my grandparents when it was all said and done. Hoping that the pain would finally go away.

And hoping that the kids wouldn't miss me too terribly.

Fifteen

Nolan
Sunday, June 30th 1:57 AM

I was sitting in the waiting room a nervous wreck. I had bit my nails down to nubs while I watched Liam and Stella playing with Legos on the floor.

They were blissfully unaware that their sister was lying in the critical unit fighting for her life. They kept asking when they would get to see Janey so they could show her what they made.

It was a wonder that they were awake to begin with.

I sighed and ran my hand through my hair. My mother was sitting next to me and she had a hand on my leg. I smiled at her quickly.

Every time I sighed or shifted in my seat, she would put her hand on my leg. As if to let me know that it would somehow be okay.

That wishful thinking got shot to shit when Dr. Kowalski walked into the waiting room looking somber and followed by an equally somber Dr. Bright.

I got to my feet and wiped my sweaty hands on my pants. Mr. and Mrs. East got to their feet as well and my parents leaned around us to look at the doctors.

"It doesn't look good," Dr. Kowalski said.

I felt my mouth go dry. I never knew why that was the typical human reaction to bad news, but my mouth was as dry as cotton.

Mrs. East started crying quietly into her husband's chest.

"What *specifically* doesn't look good," Mr. East asked.

"The lesions. They never responded to dialysis. Jane was hiding the pain she's really been in for a long time and because she never complained or said anything, she's become septic," she explained rubbing her eyes tiredly.

"Oh Aaron," Mrs. East sobbed.

I felt a pair of small arms around my leg. I looked down and saw Stella looking up at me with big sad eyes. I picked her up and she wrapped her arms and legs around me, and began to cry.

Liam was the only one out of all of us that didn't cry. I don't think he quite understood what was going on. Still, he sat there curiously listening to the doctors as they continued.

"She's fighting as much as she can. Jane's always been a very strong girl. She won't give up easily," Dr. Kowalski assured us.

"Can I see her?" I asked.

"I'm afraid not Nolan. Only immediate family can see her right now."

I felt like my world had been crushed. It didn't matter that we were supposed to get married in a few days. We weren't married *now*, which meant I couldn't see her.

I sat down, still holding Stella, unable to speak. I *needed* to see Jane. I didn't want her to think that I had abandoned her; that I didn't care.

Her parents talked to Dr. Kowalski some more before they turned to tell me that they would give her my love.

And that's when we all noticed that Liam wasn't in the room anymore.

Sixteen

Nolan
Sunday, June 30th 3:01 AM

Mom and Dad told Aaron and Jessie that they would look for Liam. They told them to go be with Jane and to send her our best.

I held onto Stella as we decided to split up and search for Liam.

I started in the lobby. I hoped he hadn't wandered there because if he had and went outside, I was afraid that I would never find him.

I went over to the information desk and asked if they had seen him. The attendant said no, but asked if I had a picture of him and she would make copies and pass it out through the hospital.

I kicked myself for not having one at that moment.

"He kind of looks like me," Stella said into my shoulder.

Then she pulled away from me and looked at the attendant, repeating herself.

"Is it okay if I take your picture, honey?" the attendant ask.

Stella nodded and told me she wanted to get down. I set her on the floor and the woman came out from behind the desk with a digital camera and held it steady for a moment. She took Stella's picture and went back around the desk.

"I'm going to email this to the entire hospital staff and tell them to be on the lookout for him," she said to us as she loaded the picture onto the computer.

I nodded in thanks and took Stella's hand.

"Let's try the parking garage," she suggested, pulling me toward the escalator.

I let her lead me around the garage before we went back into the hospital. We had spent a good twenty minutes out there checking all of the floors and stairways. When we went back inside the information attendant was waving us over.

"Yeah?" I asked stopping in front of her.

She smiled and pointed. I turned to the right and Stella pulled away from me.

"There you are!" she said, hugging her little brother. "We were so worried!"

"Thank you," I said to the woman as I made my way quickly to the children.

I couldn't quite tell who Liam had been sitting with when we arrived, but I intended to thank the man for keeping him there in that spot.

"Nolan! Look! I made a friend and he said he can marry you and you can go see Janey!" he rushed in an excited voice.

"What?" I asked in confusion.

The man stood up and held a hand out to me. That's when I noticed that he was wearing a cassock with a clerical collar. My eyes watered when I realized that Liam had left the room to find a priest.

I shook the priest's hand and he looked at me with serious eyes.

"I can't do it now. If you want to marry your fiancée I can do it in the morning during normal visiting hours."

"Please, I would greatly appreciate it," I replied tears finally spilling down my face.

He nodded and placed a hand on Liam's head, "This is a very vigilant and brave young man. I found him walking around the pediatric unit asking every adult he passed if they would 'marry' his sister. I stopped and had a chat with him out of curiosity and he told me that his biggest sister is sick in a bed upstairs and she needs to get married so she can see her boyfriend."

I picked up Liam and hugged him tightly. This little boy, unknowing how sick his sister really was, wandered the hospital for someone to be able to marry us so that I could see her.

It was the most selfless thing anyone had ever done for me in my entire life.

"Thank you, Nugget. Janey says thank you too," I said to him.

"You're welcome. Let's go build some Legos," he suggested happily.

I nodded and smiled at him.

"I need her name so I know what room to go to," the priest said to us.

"Jane East. She's in critical care."

"I'll see you tomorrow then," he said with a nod as he left.

I took Stella's hand and carried Liam toward the elevator. We waited patiently for the next car and when we stepped in, Stella pressed the button. When the doors closed, I caught a glimpse of my reflection in the doors.

Holding Liam in my arms and holding Stella's hand. I thought of the picture I had seen of Jane.

Every tear and every emotion that I had been holding in since we had arrived at the hospital finally broke me down and I sunk to the floor of the elevator crying like my world had ended.

Seventeen

Nolan
Monday, July 1st 10:07 AM

Father Lucian greeted me in the waiting room. I was so excited to see him and I got up immediately and shook his hand.

My parents were sitting with me and they each shook his hand in turn. They knew why he was there and Stella had even been brave enough to have a nurse take her to Jane's room to let her parents know that he was here.

I gave Liam to my parents when Stella returned, red faced and bravely trying not to cry, and walked with Father Lucian down the hallway to Jane's room.

"What's that?" I asked noticing a document in his hand.

"Marriage license. With as much as I hate to say this, I keep these on hand in case something like this were to happen," he replied.

I nodded and turned my attention back to the hallway. I kept my eyes forward as we passed all of the open doors. I didn't want to see other people suffering any more than I wanted to be getting married this way.

"Nolan."

I nodded at Mr. East who was half standing outside of Jane's room waiting for us.

"Father," he said, shaking the priest's hand.

"You need to be ready for what you're about to see," he said after Father Lucian went in. "Janey is very sick. She's got some tubes in her and she's hooked up to a dialysis machine. She's not very responsive but her eyes are open. Wide open. She just stares at the ceiling so I'm not sure if she's really there. She's … she's jaundiced too. I need you to be sure you want to do this and I need you to be strong enough to be in there with her. I don't know if she can see us or not, but if she can ..." his voice trailed off as his words caught in his throat.

"If I still have your blessing as well as Jessie's, I'd like to go through with this," I said quietly.

"Alright," he said as he nodded and led me into the room.

I took a deep breath and walked in. I saw her mother first, because I refused to look at her. I walked over and she stood up to give me a hug.

Then I turned my attention to the girl that I loved more than anything in the world. The girl that made me feel like anything was possible. The girl that taught me how to love unconditionally.

I felt my heart shatter into a million pieces. She wasn't the girl in the picture anymore. She wasn't the girl in the swing on that cool day in the park. She wasn't the girl that was excited to hold the Adelie Penguin.

I went over to Jane's yellow, fragile body and looked down at her. I placed a hand gently on top of her head and leaned down, kissing her as softly as I could on her now dry, cracked lips.

"Hi Janey," I whispered softly to her.

She blinked but never turned her eyes to look at me.

"I need to know who will speak for her," Father Lucian said gently.

"I will," Jessie said, getting to her feet.

He nodded and began.

"Dearly beloved, we are gathered together here in the sight of God, and in the face of this congregation, to join together this Man and this Woman in holy matrimony..."

I had made a point of holding Jane's hand through the entire thing. It was burning hot and limp, but when Father Lucian got to the part of the vows where he asked if she took me as her lawfully wedded husband, her hand tightened around mine and she coughed. I looked down at her while Jessie said “I do” in Jane’s place and her eyes were on me. I took a deep breath and smiled at her as she coughed again, tears slowly falling down the sides of her face.

Jessie gave me my ring and I slid it on. I gently put Jane’s on her hand and kept my eyes on her beautiful face.

The last thing I heard Father Lucian say was “you may now kiss the bride”. Her eyes were still on me when I turned to face her. I leaned down to kiss her and I heard her straining as she moved her face up toward me. When our lips met, she was exhausted from having moved that little bit, and her kiss was more of a quick series of puckers.

It was the most amazing, meaningful, and perfect kiss I had ever received.

“I love you,” I whispered to her.

She coughed again before turning her eyes back to the ceiling.

Seventeen

Nolan
Wednesday, July 3rd 11:01 PM

Jane had closed her eyes about ten minutes after we got married and hadn't opened them since. Father Lucian went straight to the court house to make it legal so that none of us would have to leave her bedside.

Stella would occasionally come in and sit to read her some books that were in the waiting room. Liam came in once and when he saw his beloved Starr as sick as she was, he walked right out and never came back in.

Aaron would pace the room incessantly and Jessie would periodically run a brush through Jane's hair.

I had taken up shop to her left and wild horses wouldn't be able to move me away from her side.

Around six o'clock that night, they had brought in a heart monitor. They said they needed to keep track of the beating because she wasn't as strong as she was when she first got there.

The damn beeping was driving me crazy, but I stood to reason that I would rather hear the beeping than not.

At seven they came in and took her dialysis machine out of the room.

By eight o'clock, I was paging the nurse to find out why they hadn't brought it back yet. Five minutes after that, Dr. Kowalski entered the room.

"There's no point in continuing dialysis. Her kidneys are irreparably damaged. We haven't found any donors who are a match to her bloody type and her blood pressure is through the roof. It's just a matter of how long she wants to hold on now," she said to us gently.

Aaron finally stopped pacing and sat down next to Jessie who started to cry uncontrollably. I asked him if I could bring Stella and Liam in to say goodbye to Jane and he said yes.

Liam refused. He said that he didn't want to see Jane sick and he would see her when she got home and she was doing better. Stella stood up like a big girl and held my hand all the way to the room. When she entered, she climbed the bed carefully and put her head on Jane's chest, wrapping an arm around her waist. She didn't cry until her father told her it was time for her to go back to the waiting room ten minutes later.

"I love you Janey," she shrieked over and over as he dragged her out of the room.

Nine o'clock came and went and Jane's monitor was still beeping steadily.

Jessie was still crying.

Aaron was looking out the window, with his hands in his pockets.

I was still sitting next to her.

I rolled my wedding ring around and around on my finger. Something had to give. Something had to get better. Someone as bright and loving as Jane couldn't die like this.

It wasn't fair.

Ten thirty rolled around and her heart rate started to slow down according to the monitor. Jessie burst into hysterical tears and ran from the room.

I could swear she said "I can't be here when she dies" but I wasn't eighty five percent sure.

Aaron sighed deeply and went over to Jane. He kissed her on her forehead and told her that he loved her. On his way out of the room he put a hand on my shoulder.

"I'm sorry, Nolan."

I looked up at him, "So am I."

He nodded and walked out of the room to find his wife.

I ran my thumb over the top of Jane's hand and watched her breathing becoming labored.

“If you get better, we can take that walk on the beach,” I whispered to her.

At eleven oh one, the monitor flat lined.

I was swarmed by doctors and nurses who pretty much shoved me out of the door and tried to resuscitate her.

I stood outside of her room listening to orders being yelled around and I think they almost felt as desperate as I did.

But it wasn’t their world, their love, their wife lying dead in that bed; it was mine.

Dr. Stein, who had been the attending on her case, finally came out of the room. He gave me a very somber look and put a hand on my shoulder.

“I’m sorry.”

I took a deep breath.

“Can I sit with her?”

“For a few moments, but then we have to move her,” he said.

I nodded and pushed the door open. The room was empty except for a nurse who was removing Jane's I.V.

"She just looks like she's sleeping," I said softly.

"A definite sleeping beauty," the nurse replied. "Will you be okay alone?"

"Yeah. I just want to sit here."

She nodded and walked out of the room, leaving me alone with Jane. I sat down next to her again and I ran my hand over her hair.

I wanted so desperately for her to react, to breathe, to do anything to show me that she was still alive.

But she didn't.

Her chest didn't go up and down.

Her eyes didn't blink.

And her hand, now cold, didn't squeeze mine.

"I'm glad it doesn't hurt anymore," I said. "I'm glad that you're probably in a place where you can walk anywhere you want and you're as radiant as ever. I'm glad that I got to know you and love you for the small amount of time that I did. I'm glad that I got to marry you before you left."

I felt it coming and I wasn't going to try to hold it back.

"But how the fuck am I supposed to do this without you?" I blurted out angrily.

I started to cry harder than I had in the elevator. I put my head on her stomach and let myself grieve her. Even though she had just "left" I already felt enough pain to last a thousand lifetimes.

"Nolan? It's time to go."

I recognized Dr. Bright's voice and I got to my feet without so much as a glance at him. I kissed Jane for the last time, closing my eyes tightly.

"I love you so much," I managed to say.

I walked out of her room and past the waiting room where my parents called out my name. I walked down the stairs from the eighth floor and straight out of the hospital.

I looked up bitterly at the night sky, searching for the perfect, newest Starr in Heaven.

Eighteen

Nolan
Friday, July 5th 8:00 AM

I woke up on my twenty third birthday on my parents couch. Jane's body had been brought back to Paris. Aaron had asked me if it was okay with me, I told him that I felt it was the right thing to do.

I sat up and rubbed my face.

"Good morning, sweetheart," Mom said softly.

I glanced toward the living room doorway and saw her standing there in a beautiful black dress.

"It's a great morning. We get to bury my wife," I muttered walking past her and up the stairs.

I heard her sigh heavily as I disappeared into the bathroom. I jumped in the shower and washed myself with the body wash that Jane always said she loved smelling on me. I dried myself off and stepped out of the shower to brush my teeth.

I walked into my old bedroom and sighed when I saw the dark gray suit that my mother had laid out for me.

Last night we had the memorial service for her. A lot of her family showed up. Quite a few of childhood friends, and a small group of girls our age. They looked nervous as the approached the casket, but they knelt down and paid their respects.

And as they got up and walked past me sitting in the front row, I asked them who they were.

The tall girl with the long blonde hair spoke first.

"We went to high school with her. Some losers had played a really mean joke on her and – "

"You're the cheerleading captain?" I asked quietly.

She nodded.

"Jane remembered what you did for her. She never forgot it."

Her eyes glistened and she bit her lower lip as she looked back at my Janey.

"I wish I stayed in touch with her. She seemed like such a great girl."

"She was."

"Is it okay if we stay for the service?" she asked wiping away her tears.

"Yes. Thank you for coming."

She nodded and held out a hand, "I'm Sadie."

"Nolan," I replied shaking her hand.

Sadie and her friends sat in the row behind me.

"How'd you know Jane?" she asked.

"Through marriage," I replied.

"Oh. Oh! My Gosh, I'm so sorry!" she said quickly.

"I'm not."

Stella ran past us all at that moment and hopped up on what I had dubbed the "kneeler". She leaned into the casket, hugged Jane tightly, and kissed her on the cheek, before she ran out again.

She had told me earlier that as the big sister now, she had to make sure that Liam would be okay. She was especially careful to keep him out of the room.

Sighing at the memory, I pulled on my white dress shirt and began buttoning it up as I thought of Sadie and her friends sniffling whenever someone got up and spoke about how Janey had affected their lives in one way or another.

I chose not to speak then. I would speak at the cemetery today instead.

I pulled on my pants before I grabbed my tie and began to knot it. It took me a few tries because my hands were shaking.

I saw the gold ring on my finger and sat down on the bed. Staring at it made me feel better these days and I was going to need my strength today.

Nineteen

Nolan
Friday, July 5th 10:20 AM

We left the church and were on our way to the cemetery. I was in the limo with her parents who were beyond inconsolable, my parents who were comforting her parents, and Stella and Liam sitting on either side of me.

I kept my eyes on the world outside as we made the slow procession toward Spring Grove Cemetery.

It was about a forty five minute drive, but Aaron and Jessie wanted to make sure that she would be put somewhere where no one would forget her.

I personally think it was also because they couldn't stand having her so close by without being able to see and talk to her.

Around ten twenty that morning, we rolled into the cemetery and the cars stopped, lined up behind each other.

I got out of the limo first and reached in for the children. Stella took my hand and looked at me with her sad eyes. She looked so beautiful in her little yellow sundress and white sandals, that I hated for her to have to do this.

"It'll be okay. I promise," I said to her. She nodded and turned around to take her little brother's hand.

"Come on, Nugget," she said quietly as he hopped out in his small dark blue suit and confused eyes.

"Where's Janey?" he asked suspiciously.

"She's over there," Stella said pointing at the brown shiny casket with the beautiful white and blue flower arrangement on top.

Before he had a chance to ask any more questions, she put her hand over his mouth and led him toward the rows of chairs.

Next were my parents. My mother in her black dress and my father in his dark suit. They both looked at me sadly and all I could do was nod.

Finally Aaron and Jessie emerged. Red faced and numb, they walked with my parents and took their seats in the front row.

I looked at the green, green grass for a moment.

"Nolan," a voice said.

I raised my eyes and smiled sadly. It was Father Lucian.

"Mr. and Mrs. East asked me to do the services here. I hope that's okay with you."

"I wouldn't have it any other way, Father," I replied softly.

He gave me a smile and put a hand around my shoulder as he walked me to the waiting Mourners of Jane East.

I sat down next to my parents as Father Lucian took his place at the head of Jane's casket.

The service started as he went through the Rites of Whatever and I somehow managed to block him, my parents, Jane's parents, and everyone else out who was sobbing.

I wondered if Jane could see us. I wondered if she was standing by somewhere hoping that everyone would stop crying for her. I wondered, wherever she was, if she still wore her ring as proudly as I wore mine.

My thoughts were interrupted ten minutes later when Father Lucian asked anyone if they wanted to share memories of Jane.

I put my hands on my knees and went to stand up, when Liam got up and walked over to the casket.

"Why is she in a box?" he asked innocently.

That was all it took to set Jessie off into another bout of hysterical crying.

"Because she went to Heaven," Stella said walking over to him. She put her hand on his arm to guide him back to his chair but he pulled way.

I watched him ball his fists angrily at his side and look at Stella with a bright red face.

"But ... She didn't say goodbye."

"She couldn't," Stella said quietly reaching for him again.

"When you love someone and you're going away somewhere, you're a'sposed to say goodbye!" he yelled angrily.

"Stop it," she hissed. "You're making mom cry."

"I don't care! She should have said goodbye!" he yelled throwing himself on the grass.

I got up and walked over to him. I knelt in the grass next to this hysterical little boy who didn't understand quite yet what had happened to his oldest sister.

"She didn't say goodbye to me either, Liam. But that doesn't mean she loved us any less. Janey always told me how proud she was of you because you're such a big boy. Can you be that big boy now? For Janey?" I asked helping him to his knees.

He nodded and got to his feet. He was still crying and he threw his arms around telling me that he wanted to go with his sister.

"Me too. But we can't. We have to be strong, okay?"

He pulled away from me and ran back to his father, climbing into his lap and crying harder than ever.

Father Lucian asked if anyone else had anything to say. My speech was burning a hole in my inner pocket, but I decided against reading it. Nothing I could possibly say right now would be consoling to anyone.

When the time finally came to lower her into the ground, I walked away. It was bad enough to lose her, but if I actually saw them do it, it would be "final".

So I stood on top of a hill next to a mausoleum with an angel out front while they put my Jane into the ground.

Twenty

Nolan
Monday, August 5th 1:43 PM

"I hope you like your headstone. It took us forever to decide on what to do. Aaron thought that it should say Jane Ransom and I thought that it should say Jane East. He said it deserved to say Ransom because we were married and that's what you would have wanted, but I guess we'll never know.

"I ... Jane, there was something I wanted to read to you the day we buried you but I couldn't do it. Not with Liam becoming aware of what happened to you, so if you have some time I wanted to read it to you today. I added some stuff to it too.

"Well, here it goes.

"'My Dearest Love,

I'm sorry that we never got to take that walk on the beach. I'm sorry that we never even made it to the bathroom. I'm sorry that you suffered and I'm sorry that I couldn't save you.

You were the most amazing thing that ever happened to me and I selfishly wanted to do anything I could to keep you here for as long as I could. I was blind to your pain and suffering and I'll never forgive myself for it.

I can only hope that wherever you are, you still love me and know in your heart that I will always love you.

No one will ever take your place, and I'll carry the memory of you forever in my heart.

I never truly thanked you for coming into my life. I may have only known you for a short time, but it was the most amazing time of my life.

Stella told me that she'll take care of Liam, so you won't have to worry about either of them.

Liam wanted me to tell you that he's not mad anymore. He understands now that you couldn't say goodbye and he wants you to know that he's sorry for being mad.

Aaron and Jessie are doing a little bit better. They kept your wheelchair and put it in your room. No one's allowed to go in there; it's exactly the way you left it.

Mom and Dad visit them everyday and sometimes I go over there too.

Sadie visits me sometimes. She wants to make sure that I'm okay and that you know that she never forgot you.

I just wanted to end this by saying that the world was a lucky place to have you in it and that twenty one years of Jane was more than enough for it.

But it will never be enough for me.

I love you so much."

I put the paper back into my pocket and looked up at the sky as a cool breeze went by.

Wherever she was, she heard me.

Made in the USA
San Bernardino, CA
04 September 2014